LAW FIRMS

&

LIBRARIANS

THE FILE OF DREAD

Adventure # 1

By T Oliver Courtney

Copyright 2023 Thomas Courtney

All rights reserved. No part of this publication may be reproduced or transmitted in any form or by any means, electronic or mechanical, including photocopy, or any information storage and retrieval system, without permission from the publisher.

ISBN: 9798859304837
Independently published.

Dedication

To the humans: Hanah, Ben, Brittany, Kaitlyn, and Spencer. Thank you for all the time we've spent together on our incredible adventures. Both worlds, the real, and the fantastical, are made better when you are in them.

For the Players

Welcome to the Tiki Mermaid, a proud establishment on the fog shrouded hills of San Deego Bay. It's a place where locals go to "chill" even on a warm summer day. Tonight, the town is alive with activity, as the city streets are packed for a customary festival known as *Sinkody Miyoh*. You've arrived at just the right time to find employment, or just to celebrate over a pint of good brew. It's the finest night in the finest city.

Or is it? Rumors of an ancient and sinister evil that once dwelt in the heart of the city have always been a part of local lore. But now there is talk that local "real" estate issues may be to blame. Could a *develloper* still lurk in the underpinnings of shadowy legal dealings? Businesses rise, and businesses disappear, without a trace. Could this ancient menace have returned?

Only you can solve the dark and mysterious plot of The File of Dread. Weave your way through *comic book shops, amusement parks* and *law firms*. Visit a *conspiracy theorist* or a *barista* collecting clues. Collect and use a variety of more and more powerful logic as your character levels up in this world of reality.

Included in this module is a 32 page appendix with seven new logical items, three new opponents not found in either the Man Manual, or The Female

Folio, including: *Sror tee sister*, four new types of *preppy*, and the dreaded *greater real estate develloper*.

Choose from two new sub-classes of logic-user: *craft-beer loving hipster* or *legal analyst*. Or become a local athletic: *surfer*, *skateboarder*, or *Lah Hoynian tennis coach*. Each is complete with different backgrounds and skills to choose from, all compatible with L&L's West Coast Campaign Guidebook.

Matilda, the proprietor of the Tiki Mermaid, has just tapped a new keg filled with eyes, peas and hay. And she needs people, *real* people, to drink it while they still can.

Contents

Prologue

LEVEL 1

Chapter 1 *The Tiki Mermaid*

Chapter 2 *The Dea Jay's Jacket of Narcissism, Plus Two*

Chapter 3 *Social and Emotional Damage*

Chapter 4 *A First Kiss of the Humankind*

Chapter 5 *Potions of Monster Energy and a Hoop of Hill Giant Hula*

Chapter 6 *The Battle of the Five Sror-Tee Sisters*

Chapter 7 *Total Party Bill*

Level 2

Chapter 8 *A Level 5 Conspiracy Theorist*

Chapter 9 *The Great Tomithino*

Chapter 10 *I Wish a Carron Would*

Chapter 11 *The Legend of Skay Ting*

Chapter 12 *Lair of the Ancient Silver*

Chapter 13 *Deuce Brockit, the Surf Rocket*

Chapter 14 *A Billion Deaths Served*

CHAPTER 15 *Save Versus Advertisement*

Chapter 16 *Save Versus Snackage*

Chapter 17 *Quest for the Smart Foan*

Appendix A: L&L Adversaries

Appendix B: New Logical Items

Appendix C: New Player Characters
Appendix D: Suggestions for Future Play

Prologue

Dear Human,

If you enjoy roleplaying games such as Dungeons & Dragons, you're in the right place! But what if you are new to this type of adventure? If so, you need have no fear, or what you call in your world-*stress*. All you need is your imagination.

For example, picture right now in your mind a group of fantastical creatures sitting around a large table-shaped boulder. The boulder and the creatures are in the middle of a rather lovely swamp. There is a pixie, a faun, an ogre, and even a unicorn.

Just like you, these magical beasts use their imagination in *their* world to play games.

Tonight's game is called Law Firms & Librarians.

The ogre has decided to become the Library Master. He will describe all of the setting and the action of the story to the other players. Each of them in turn will be pretending to play a type of human from our world. Like Dungeons & Dragons, they will act out their characters and try to solve a perilous mystery. They will roll dice and use information they read about to decide what to do, and what to say, in their game.

One has decided to play a surfer. One has chosen legal assistant. A third is very excited about a new class he has read about, beer-loving hipster. They've been warned that danger is imminent. A terrible thing, known as a "file" is about to open, spewing forth a horde of evil consequences for all in this great city of San Deego, here in the realm of Merrah Kah. They must use all of their cunning, wits and creativity to stop it.

The Library Master has just placed their character's game figures on top of the boulder. The sounds of the swamp have faded into the night.

The adventure is about to begin!

LEVEL 1

Chapter 1

The Tiki Mermaid

UTAH: I walk into the bar on my two legs. I sit down and I order a huge beer. Its golden wheat with a hint of red-tinted amber and froth slides down along the cold glass where it pools on the lacquered wood. Half of the pint sloshes down the front of my garments—a *Haw Wine shirt*, red with white flowers, blue *surftrunks*, and *flip flops*. Now I'm all wet. Right where my two legs meet. That's called a *crotch* right?

LM: Correct. You can also call it your junk, privates, and family jewels.

UTAH: I get none of that by the way. But thanks. Good to know for future humans.

LM: The bartender asks you if you'd like another beer.

UTAH: What does he look like?

LM: It's a she actually.

UTAH: Oh cool. My first female. I wink at her. That's one eye only I believe.

LM: Congratulations. You've succeeded on your first flirtation attempt. You can learn her name now if you like. Besides, she's got a name tag that she keeps pinned to her bar apron.

UTAH: That's a first. Can I read the runes?

LM: Yes, you can read them. They spell out the name: M-A-T-I-L-D-A. The female human before you is the owner and operator. And she's pretty. Easy on both of your eyes as the people say. She's quick too. She puts a glass here. Pours a shot there. Bottles flip up. End over end like a spell was cast, back in their proper places. She reaches back to tap a keg while she's taking an order from another guy at the end of the bar, snatching his words in mid-air over the raucous laughter (Yeah, that's you, hang on). Then she whirls around, wipes the froth off a pint. Sends the ale sliding down to a third fellow. (Yes, that one is yours). All seamless.

UTAH: Reality is so neat.

LM: Did I mention she was pretty? She's got gorgeous, curly hair locks that fall against her cheeks, right at her perky little nose. That's cute here.

UTAH: Is she brun–?

LM: Brunette? No. She's blonde so your modifier won't work.

UTAH: It's so lame how important color is to humans sometimes.

LM: She leans over the bar, looks at you with both of her eyes and gives you just a hint of her two breasts.

UTAH: Do I like that?

LM: Yes, you do. She says, "You thirsty kid?"

UTAH: I find that weird since I'm technically at the *young adult* stage, right?

LM: I suppose you probably would. A bit. But remember she's a bartender class.

UTAH: I thought she was a barista?

LM: Same thing to you right now. They kind of take this approach with everybody especially when they're in their lair.

12

UTAH: I totally say yes to a beer then, and I order one for the girl next to me. Want to make her jealous of this new opportunity to potentially mate.

LM: Well, Matilda's class is immune to jealousy, remember? Besides, that's not a girl sitting next to you. It's another man, like you, and he's got a big bushy conditioned beard, which is like upside down hair on the face. He is wearing a t-shirt too, only his has runes written on it.

UTAH: Runes on a garment? Weird. Can I read it?

LM: Yep. These read, "Fast Times At Ridge Man, Hi."

UTAH: I say *hi* back. Do I know what a ridge man is yet?

LM: No.

UTAH: Well, then I tell him to enjoy that beer I just bought him. Might lead to something, right? I drink my second beer. How am I feeling?

LM: Pretty good. You've got a high tolerance for eyes, pees, and hay.

UTAH: Do I know why they put all that in their beer?

LM: Yes. Mixed they make a type of light ale that people in this part of the world drink especially when the weather is fair.

UTAH: Sounds like magic.

SPENCER: Beer is magical in any land.

UTAH: Right? I want another.

SPENCER: Me too.

KAITLYN: And me.

UTAH: Do I see the others yet?

LM: No.

UTAH: I'm scrying the joint then.

KAITLYN: You mean, *scanning*. Humans *scan*.

LM: **Okay. How so?**

UTAH: You know. I'm watching for clues and shit.

LM: Ok, well first there is no shit unless you check the bathrooms. For clues, hang on. Welcome to the Tiki Mermaid. Matilda, the proprietor, welcomes you with hair as fair as her golden craft brew and a voice as sweet as honey. Around you, sitting on their buttocks, are many groups of humans engaged in lively chit-chat. Some are dressed in *pants* and *long sleeve buttoned shirts* with *ties* (Yes, that indicates they just came from an *office*. That's explained in your adventure background and in the appendix.) Others are wearing *t-shirts*, or *Haw Wine shirts*. Most

of the females are wearing leggings. Lots of skin showing.

UTAH: Why do the females show more skin?

LM: It's just a human thing.

SPENCER: Man Manual says that men have poor imaginations. What's imagination got to do with it I wonder?

LM: Yeah. Okay, well the most interesting feature of the bar is that there's a huge mermaid themed fresco behind the counter where you are currently leaning. It's a floor to ceiling image, a woman with a fish tail, being chased by sea animals at play. She looks a lot like Matilda, and it's obvious that whoever the artist was tried unsuccessfully to copy her likeness. The mermaid's holding a glass of beer. So are the sea animals, beers in their flippers, in crab claws. Stuff like that.

UTAH: That's really weird that there's a freaking mermaid on their bar wall. Total fantasy punk. I love it.

LM: Hang on, there's more. Hundreds of potion bottles are stacked on shelves in front of the painting. Also, humans do a lot of talking, so the place is loud, plus there is music playing.

UTAH: Who is playing music? I mean where are they?

LM: There isn't anyone playing. It's from a *speaker*. That's a little box that plays music in this world.

UTAH: Music from a box. Okay. How is that even logic?

LM: Trust me, it is.

UTAH: Well, fine. Do I see any groups that look like a particularly bad ass?

LM: I told you, no other creatures allowed in human bars, only humans.

UTAH: I meant *badass* from the jargon section of the Man Manual.

LM: Oh, sorry. Nice work, using the lingo by the way. Well, now that you mention it there is one rather *badass* group. All of them have the same hairstyle on their heads, which is common for parties of the same class.

UTAH: Do I recognize the class?

LM: Yeah, judging by their sunburnt faces and bleached hair, you're pretty sure they're *surfers*. Plus, they're calling each other *bro* a lot and all of them have flip flops and Haw Wine shirts. Different colors than yours though.

UTAH: Nice! My homies.

LM: No. That's dea jay slang.

KAITLYN: You should go discuss the tide chart with them. We can find out more about any water issues they're having. Time to collect clues people, otherwise we're just roleplaying tonight. I want real debate. Smack and trash!

UTAH: Got lots of time... Besides, I'm thinking this time we should take a slower approach. How many times have we done this where we rush into some quest, without even considering our options?

SPENCER: Not a bad point, I must admit it.

LM: Ok then, so what are you all doing?

UTAH: Me? I'm drinking this beer. Low profile. Peeking over the top of the glass like. We got surfers, we got a bartender. So far so good team. Hey, what do I look like again?

LM: You're average for a human male. Well, a tad shorter. Adult males in this part of the world are a bit heavier usually so you're considered undersized. You've got long blond hair, but since you're a surfer class, it doesn't immediately confuse you as a female. You're still in what they call the late stages of adult puberty. You have two eyes, two ears, one mouth, two arms, two legs.

UTAH: Fingers? Toes?

LM: Yep. Ten each. Hands *and* feet.

UTAH: Cool.

KAITLYN: Do I have hair on my head too?

LM: Yes.

KAITLYN: Then we all do?

SPENCER: Not me.

UTAH: I actually read that it goes away. Are you older than me?

KAITLYN: Something called *pube hurty,* right? Not sure what the pube thing is or how much it hurts though.

LM: No, I'm pretty sure the chart showed you kept head hair for a few more levels. Let me check…Yep, called "middle-age." You have to be older, so no, sorry, you have head hair. By the way, It's all there, friends. You gotta pay attention. You're slowing down the story now.

LM: Listen up, let's get back on the trail here. There are three of you, right? You're all sitting at a bar. You're in the downtown area of San Deego. Its nighttime. The bar is crowded. Two of you got blonde hair, on your head. Same as the bartender. Same color as your ale.

UTAH: I'm pretty sure it's *Sandy Go*. Because of the beach on the map.

LM: Stop it. I just told you how to pronounce it and it's San Deego. Your name is--

UTAH: Huh?

LM: "What in the snakeskin is your name, seriously? You had time."

UTAH: I know my name. Hang on. Its…its Utah…Utah Spicolli.

SPENCER: That's a total rip off. We said we weren't going to do that.

KAITLYN: You got that from a surfer name generator, right?

LM: Okay *Utah*. You're an eighteen-year-old male. You've got an injury to part of your body, your skin, due to excessive sun damage. Just making sure you know that ahead of time in case you're in the sun again today.

SPENCER: Ouch.

UTAH: Right?

LM: And you've got a massively short attention span because of your *societal presence* modifier. But you're a *surfer*, which we've already been over. This class fits in well with a variety of financially unstable humans. Its definitely helping you at the bar because

of the local area's lack of economic input. You've got a thing for brunettes too.

UTAH: That's the ones with brown hair right?

LM: And you've just splashed beer all down the front of your trousers, and that part is *not* helping you fit in.

UTAH: I seriously do not get that.

KAITLYN: Oh. Do me! My name is Kaitlyn Jacoby and I have a tabby named Meyers. He is hiding outside the bar right now because apparently some Library Masters are rule-lawyers for allowing cats to go to bars in Sandy Go. Also, I have no wings, and my skin is all one color, definitely not translucent, purple or sparkly, and my ears are not pointy. Also, I go by Kaitlyn Esquire sometimes if I feel like it because that tells people right away that I can be a legal hero. If anyone needs that sort of thing.

LM: It's San Deego. And you aren't going to find any legal stuff just yet, so hold Spencer's tail. Further, we already talked about how weird it would be to bring your pet into another bar. Finally, yes, familiars in bars was home-ruled seasons ago.

UTAH: I don't get that either.

LM: In human society people do *not* bring their familiars with them to bars. Unless they are blind.

UTAH: In both eyes?

LM: Yes.

SPENCER: I thought you could also have a familiar in a bar if you were deaf.

KAITLYN: In both ears?

LM: Wyvern's poison. Can I continue?

KAITLYN: Go on.

UTAH: Go on.

SPENCER: Go on.

LM: Well, Kaitlyn Jacoby, you're a female. You're considered *attractive* because of your physique modifier. You have braided hair like a centaur's tail at festival. It's a sort of wheat and strawberry mix in hue. You're a bit older than Utah here, but that has only increased your attraction modification. You walked in alone on two legs, Meyers successfully hidden, and that typically means you'll have just a few rounds before you're surrounded by various human males, so consider what you want to do a bit quickly.

KAITLYN: Good. Let the adventure come to me. Right?

UTAH: Ha. Cause that worked so good when we were in that inn in Lost Ambulance. Remember?

SPENCER: Can I introduce myself now?

LM: Yeah, just so long as we're clear that you all haven't met yet.

SPENCER: Finally. Howdy, bar patronizing humans. I'm Spencer McAdams. I actually am a *first level Brewmaster*, which is a subclass of *hipster*, so I know *a lot* about the beer at this bar right now. I've got loads of hair too, right?

LM: Yeah, everywhere except on the very top of your head.

SPENCER: Oh good. At least one of us is normal around here.

LM: You have a big bushy red beard which grows from the bottom part of your face, and true, you love beer which gives you a plus two to detect ingredient origin, not that this will be important.

SPENCER: I think that's a clue!

LM: Whatever. McAdams, you definitely are fitting in the best here. Utah and Kaitlyn just think they are in their element right now. But you're doing way better so try not to screw anything up yet.

SPENCER: Cool. I want to sniff Utah's crotch to see what kind of beer he was drinking.

UTAH: I'll sniff his crotch right back, please.

LM: NOOOOO!!!!!!! This is not what Sandy Goans do! I've shared this with you all. You animals need to read the adventure brief.

KAITLYN: I believe it's 'you people'?

SPENCER: I don't remember reading anything against sniffing a cr—

LM: Fine. You sniff each other's crotches. I'm assuming you are doing this too.

KAITLYN: Of course. Never separate the party when they are sniffing crotches, am I right team?

LM: Well, congratulations. You've now been noticed by the entire staff of Tiki Mermaid, as well as all the patronage. And no one looks happy with any of you.

KAITLYN: Love that name by the way.

SPENCER: I stand up, throw my coins down on the bar and shout that I am buying beers for the whole place. And I use my beer modifier to identify the good stuff. Bang. Back in business.

LM: Those coins don't even pay for your own beer! Didn't any of you check the converter?

SPENCER: What do you mean?

LM: Coins here work differently. You want the type of money that folds, remember?

UTAH: Dragon Shit. In what world do coins not buy beers?

SPENCER: Apparently, the *real* one.

Chapter 2

The Dea Jay's Jacket of Narcissism, Plus Two

KAITLYN: How does one fold a coin anyway?

LM: The foldable stuff is made of paper. Some money is coins, but they aren't worth much. The better stuff is paper.

KAITLYN: That can burn though.

LM: Again, we've been over this. Not a lot of fire here. They got something called *lick trissity.*

KAITLYN: I'll bet they do.

SPENCER: That's what the faerie said.

LM: Point is, you all can barely pay for your own beers now. Thanks to Spicolli here, you've used up the last of your petty savings you got from that *gardener* **when you defeated her weeds and poisoned ivy.**

UTAH: Those little suckers put up a good fight, too. Knew we should have asked for more upfront. Money that folds. Gotta remember that. Not to mention carrying around all these copper coins has been a real pain in my two buttocks.

SPENCER: Well, now what do we do? I just bought a whole keg.

LM: You *ordered* **a whole keg. It is now getting tapped and poured into glasses around the bar. You haven't bought it yet.**

KAITLYN: We could try and fly away. Disappear?

LM: This is Law Firms & Librarians. Think less magical, more logical.

KAITLYN: Oh right. I keep forgetting that. Well, what about a diversion?

SPENCER: How do we screw things up so quick?

LM: No idea. Say, why don't you all think. Play to your strengths.

UTAH: Well, I can't surf here. Kaitlyn's attractiveness got cancelled by her crotch sniffing. And Spencer's beer knowledge isn't going to mean chimera spit when the bar finds out we can't pay for his round.

KAITLYN: Play to our weaknesses?

UTAH: Which is?

LM: Right now? Utah's attention span and the fact he brought his surfboard inside the bar didn't help either. I told you; you can't just stroll into bars all geared up. Plus, it looks like he urinated on himself.

UTAH: Which is not attractive?

LM: No. Plus you just saw a clue which if you'd like to hear it, might explain that none of that is doing much for you.

UTAH: Wait. I saw a clue? I knew it!

LM: Yep. I was going to tell you about it, but we keep getting into backstory. And the more you guys consult your guidebooks instead of just roleplay—

UTAH: What did I see?

LM: There's a group of people, three males, sitting together on their two buttocks in chairs near you.

SPENCER: The surfers?

LM: Nope. This group is different. They're calling each other things like *homie* and *home-skillet*. They're still wearing their glasses of sun shielding inside the bar even though there's no sun right now.

KAITLYN: So fantastic.

UTAH: What do they look like?

LM: Well, humans all share many features except some come in slightly different colors. But imagine that the leader sort of looks like a tortle, small head poking out of a golden shell. Except the golden shell is actually a thick jacket, painted in gold leaf. Under the jacket, you can see golden jewelry encrusted with magnificent gems around his neck. He wears golden rimmed glasses over his eyes. This fine fellow is bookended by two cream-colored followers in white t-shirts that have no sleeves. Each wear plenty of their own neck jewelry, and have various runes and symbols shaved into their head hair.

KAITLYN: Woah.

UTAH: I try to listen.

SPENCER: It's so weird that they use one chair for both buttocks, right?

LM: Well, it's noisy. And there's that strange local music and people speaking Eng Lish loudly to one another. So, you can't hear much. But they are each pulling their lips upward, showing their teeth. And they are pointing one finger at all your crotches. That's pretty much how you noticed them because they noticed you.

KAITLYN: Ever notice how a human's happy expression looks a lot like a horse in pain?

LM: The tortle-like human male who is wearing a golden garment is slapping one of his knees with his hand. Now that he's facing you, you see he's got even more massive gold jewelry under this golden garment than you thought possible.

KAITLYN: Remember team, that's called *bling* and although it's the source of much power, it is often cursed. Once worn, it's near impossible to take it off and makes your *self-steam* drop through the canopy.

LM: Right. Nice research. He's pointing his finger directly at your face now.

UTAH: What does it mean to point one finger?

LM: Depends. Finger and hand gestures are in your guidebook by the way.

SPENCER: Swamp moss. Says here that means "there is something noticeable and could be positive or negative." The hand on the knee could be a sign he's exhausted.

UTAH: Humans don't usually attack with their teeth. My notes say that this group is happy.

KAITLYN: Sweet buttercup nectar! Then, we've just made some friends—

UTAH: Our first friends—

SPENCER: Who can help us buy some beer! I'll walk over to try and persuade them. I talk to the people with the gold garment on his body.

LM: The garment is called a jacket. Not needed in San Deego so this is clearly for sexual display and physical enhancement. A golden dea-jay jacket. Check your guidebook for a visual. Puffy. Makes him look heavily muscled and helps him stand out. He's still smiling. And it's *person*. One people is person.

UTAH: Got it. Wow guys, a dea jay already! I told you this adventure was the sprite's tights. Ok, let's do this! I say in Eng Lish, "What's up, my main *man*." Then, I point my finger at him and smile too.

SPENCER: Nice! Someone's been reading their Humans and History.

LM: Yeah, I'm throwing you a plus three on that local use of phrase. Another +2 for class lingo. Well done. Where do you point?

UTAH: His crotch.

LM: Ouch, that actually is not an acceptable human hand gesture.

UTAH: Come on. It doesn't say anything about where the gestures go! Besides, they were doing it to us!

LM: Not everything is in the guidebook. This is L&L. You have to use your realism.

UTAH: I know. I know. Okay, well what happens?

LM: He says something in Eng Lish to his friends.

UTAH: Which is?

LM: "I think this little freak likes my schlong, homies." Basically, he thinks you are admiring his genitalia. What do you say back?

UTAH: That depends. Are they admirable?

LM: Possibly.

UTAH: I tell him in Eng Lish. "Yes Sir, I do."

SPENCER: I walk over now too and I ask him if I can sniff his prodigious genitalia.

KAITLYN: Meh, I'll go too.

LM: He stands up on both legs. He takes off his jacket and puts it on the table. You notice he's a lot thinner, so clearly this jacket was used for physical display. Also, you can see his *underwear* because he is

saggin'. He says to Spencer, "You tryna' to start something?"

SPENCER: "Yes, I'd like to start a friendship. Nice underwear, my *muchacho*. I'm Spencer. This is Kaitlyn and that is Utah. My friends and I were wondering if you'd care to pay folding money for the beer we just ordered. We offer to pay the next round." What am I getting from his crotch?

LM: Nothing much. Hint of feces.

UTAH: What are you doing, Spencer?

SPENCER: Bluffing team. That jacket has got to be a logical item, I just know it.

LM: The dea jay laughs, "'Well, what an introduction! Sup ma bitches! I'm Lazlo. And my friends and I had a few things to do tonight. But we've decided beating your ass is going to be first on the to-do list.

KAITLYN: A to-do list. These humans think of everything, right?

UTAH: He means our buttocks. I just looked it up.

SPENCER: Oh! Or I can challenge him to a bar game. There's a whole section in Humans and History about card games. I've got a *stack of cards* in my equipment by the way. It was nonlogical, came with my class. It was either that or I could have chosen something called a lap-top, but I wasn't sure if I'd have a lap.

LM: Okay, well while you three are trying to figure out your gear, the dea-jay's bookend friends stand up next to him. It's time to roll for initiative, people!

UTAH: Wow! We're not even out of the bar yet!

LM: McAdams, you got the beat on the dea-jay and his plus two. Spicolli, you'll be after the baddies here. Lucky for you guys Lazlo doesn't get lair actions. Dea-jays are nasty in their lairs.

UTAH: Jacoby, you know what they say about lawyers, right?

KAITLYN: That we get a plus two to bluffing when our lips are moving?

LM: You people better focus. Or else I'm going to fail your first concentration roles automatically.

SPENCER: Okay, well I'm not going tail to tail with a dea-jay first thing, lair or not. I'll grab the nearest beer components to create a wall of froth.

UTAH: A wall of what?

SPENCER: Froth. It'll give you all a turn before they attack.

LM: Okay, well based on your roll, you create a shimmering golden streak of ale appearing in the air

between you and the lead dea jay. He yells, "You fucks are going to pay for…!" But before he finishes, beer splashes across his chest in a golden shower of ale. He's stunned momentarily and his social presence is halved. His homies all failed their concentration checks watching him, so they are stunned too. Well done McAdams! Spicolli, you're next!

UTAH: I reach back to grab my surfboard.

LM: If you are going to try to use that thing as a weapon, it's not going to matter whether you are proficient with it or not.

UTAH: No. I'm totally about getting out of here and I'm not leaving without my gear again. I grab my board and look for the nearest exit. I suggest you all come with me. Otherwise, we'll need two quests just to pay off that keg and the bar damage!

SPENCER: I'm in. But, while Spicolli is doing that, I'm going to try and gallop for the dea jay's jacket. Then high step back as far as I can.

LM: What you want to do here is lunge. Humans, with only two feet, lunge. You succeed! The jacket is yours!

KAITLYN/SPENCER/UTAH: Words up! Booze yeah! Dude!

LM: Kaitlyn, you are top of the order.

KAITLYN: I'm holding my action until Spicolli, and McAdams, knows what in the hair of a human's head they are doing.

LM: Well, unfortunately, that is going to be after the dea jay, who has cleared his eyes of beer froth and can tell that McAdams has his jacket. The dea jay then grabs a glass mug by the handle, hits it against the table, which breaks the edges in jagged shards. Then, he uses his rap battle class ability to strengthen his crew's loyalty modifier. They now all have a +4 to any competition or physical attacks that involves fists, kicks, lyrics, spinning records, or yo' mama jokes. And he's got his eyes locked onto Jacoby now standing behind Spicolli. Your move, Utah.

UTAH: First, everyone stay together and get behind something. We get hit by a single beer-mug attack and we're going to have another ambulance incident. Kaitlyn's not immune to medical bills until she's a seventh level attorney. I will swing around, so I can get an exit strategy. I'm also looking for condoms to drop on the ground behind us.

LM: That's *condiments*. Very common mistake actually. There's some green paste in a bowl next to some chips, looks slippery. You can knock some over as a minor action if you want.

UTAH: Yes, please!

LM: Congratulations then, as part of your surfer subclass you can also create a reaction while holding

your surfboard. Since the dea jay and his friends entered your space they have to roll and…wow. They all failed! Your board spins around and knocks them all prone.

UTAH: I yell, "Gnarly!"

LM: Your character's first battle cry. Remind me to reward you with some reality points for that one. And wait. Your turn isn't over yet!

UTAH: There's more?
LM: Oh yeah. As you spin, looking for an exit, your two eyes lock onto something behind Matilda, past two swinging bar doors. She's the barback, which is—

KAITLYN: We have those in our world too! It's the creature, uh, human, that keeps the shelves stocked and helps the bartender. I flitted around an old tavern on the outskirts—

LM: In this case, she is a brunette human female in your zone of breeding compatibility!

UTAH: I already know I like those.

LM: Hush. There's more. But I need a concentration roll from you to unlock the mystery.

UTAH: Since we're about to get slammed in The Slammer for ordering beer we can't buy or getting put in another ambulance and losing all our loot to a health provider? I'll do it.

LM: Well then, Utah Spicolli's eyes, both, are fixated on the attractive brunette putting away glasses behind the back of the bar. This barback female is younger than Matilda and she is standing in what looks like the back of a supply room. She's reaching up to put some glasses in a high cabinet. She's turned away from you.

UTAH: Tail?

LM: For the thousandth time, humans have no tails. But her shirt is riding up, about to expose her undergarments.

UTAH: Females wear undergarments too?

LM: Yes. And continuing…she's a female, with undergarments, and she's reaching up higher and higher. Her shirt slides up. You see her belt, that's an item that holds up her trousers. It's sort of like a bridle for creatures with man-legs. And then there's something else.

UTAH: What is it?!

LM: There's what looks like runes on her skin.

UTAH: *On* her skin?

LM: Yep.

UTAH: *Weeeeeeeiiiiirrrrrd.* Are they glowing?

LM: No.

UTAH: Do I know what they say?

LM: Well, do you speak Span Lish?

UTAH: Span Lish? I thought the locals here spoke Eng Lish?

LM: They do. But some speak Span Lish from the land of Mecks Icko too. It's the next realm over. Check your map.

UTAH: Well okay. But what do the runes tell me?

LM: All you are getting is, "A key poppy". But you don't know what it means, nor are you certain what language it is. Could be Eng Lish. Could be Span Lish mixed with Eng Lish.

UTAH: Could be troglodyte. Pickles.

KAITLYN: Wait! A key poppy? I'm pretty sure that is Eng Lish. A key is a key obviously, and a poppy-says here in the Calley Phornia Campaign Guide that a poppy is a type of flower. Very pretty, but delicate.

LM: Again. It could be either Eng Lish or Span Lish actually, you can't tell. Remember that both cultures have roots in the region and sometimes words get inter-mingled—just like Ogre and Hill Giant.

UTAH: This has to mean something important then. Every key has a door, right?

KAITLYN: And behind the door must be something delicate, and beautiful. Like treasure! Hey, I forgot that I speak Span Lish!

LM: So?

KAITLYN: So, I can tell Utah if it's Span Lish!

LM: No, you can't. How are you gonna help Utah read runes in a language that he doesn't understand which you can't see yourself from the position you are still in? Not to mention you are engaged in bar debate to a dea jay and two lesser club beatboys, or at the very least its bordering now on a rap battle, all at this very moment. That's a negative.

KAITLYN: So, then what do we do?

LM: I don't know. What do you do? Look, I can't give you hints here obviously but I can at least show Kaitlyn the image from the appendix since she speaks Span Lish.

KAITLYN: Hey hey! If there's an image in the appendix, then that rune is important!

LM: Ok, just you. Here is what it looks like.

KAITLYN: Means nothing special to me, just same sound with different letters. Is the brunette doing anything else?

LM: Yeah, she turns back and gives a wink to Utah. Then she walks through a set of bar doors, and she's gone from sight.

UTAH: Do I know what a wink means?

LM: It's either because there's something in her eye, or she likes you. Generally speaking. You can always roll.

UTAH: Crit, people!! This 20 is all natural.

LM: Nice!!!! You get everything! First, you're getting a sense that something else is going down here that you all didn't really figure out yet. She may also be giving you a heads up that there's an escape out the back of the bar. Finally, since it's a crit you are 99.9% positive that she would consider you attractive.

KAITLYN: Snake tongues and hag skin! All that from blinking an eye? People are so complex.

UTAH: I'm going to jump over the bar. Follow her. If the adventure doesn't come to you, then go grab it by the head horns, right?

SPENCER: Except that you're jumping a bar while its coming to us right now.

KAITLYN: This feels like how we bottomed out our social stats in the star buck in that town called Saddle.

SPENCER: We just started too.

UTAH: If you two want to stay in the meadow, and pay for a quest's supply of beer, or see if the dea jay will let you give him his logical item back, be my guest. I'm leavin' this here watering hole, cowboys!

LM: I remember that. It's the retreat cry from A Texan in Tea Jay!

KAITLYN: I'm jumping the bar too. It's like flying for a little bit without wings, right?

SPENCER: I too wish to trot jump the bar. I'll simultaneously wave goodbye to Sir Dea—

UTAH: It's time to find out what a key poppy means, and maybe we'll find the treasure that's behind the door it unlocks!

Chapter 3

Social and Emotional Damage

LM: Bursting through the door into the back supply room of the Tiki Mermaid, you come upon a brunette human young adult female who is standing in the middle of the 10 x 10 snout chamber. Lining every wall around you, scattered on shelves floor to ceiling are potion bottles of every description and color. Each has a label. There are several tables against the north and east wall where human food is mixed and made in bowls and on plates. There are also several *com pewters* on a small desk at the west wall. Past that desk, there is a small door from which you can sense a small breeze. There are a few signs on the wall in Eng Lish. One says, "Welcome to our shit show." The other sign which hangs next to the door you just walked through, reads, "Warning. No stupid people beyond this point!" The room smells a little like vomit and pickles.

SPENCER: Eww. Pickles.

UTAH: I hope we pass through okay. Do we?

KAITLYN: Does the sign say what time the show is? Sounds like fun if we get out of this mess.

UTAH: What does this human female look like up close?

LM: Sure, her attraction modifier is quite high, and she has a sort of cedar bark skin, slightly darker than yours or Jacoby's. Her eyes are green like pond moss in the sun.

UTAH: Sounds like an elf. Does she have pointy ears?

LM: There are no elves in the real world, remember? Unless of course you encounter a level 6 cosplayer.

UTAH: What's she doing, just standing there?

LM: Nope. As soon as you all enter, she rushes behind you to the door, closes and locks it behind you. There's a pounding on the other side, and you can hear dea jay slang and cursing. "You look so familiar," she says.

UTAH: I say, "Hey chicken."

LM: It's chick. You don't say chicken unless she is scared. She says, "Oh my god, you guys really pissed off Lazlo."

UTAH: "Actually, I pissed *on* myself, miss," I say. I'm going to give her back a wink. Then, I'll paw the ground with my hooves.

LM: You don't have hooves.

UTAH: Oh right, I push out my chest then. I still got one of those right?

LM: Yep.

UTAH: Then, I say, "How are you called?"

LM: She looks at your surfboard first, Utah. Her eyes narrow. This is a human sign she either sees something she likes, or she is upset. "I'm Selena. Is that a 6-10 Tony Staples with a triple stringer?"

UTAH: "6-8," I say back quickly. "I like the 6-8 better with a triple." Then I blink. Twice. People, this female is completely into me! I ask her where the key is? Also, I was just reading that a poppy is a local flower. So, I ask her if she knows about that flower, too.

LM: That's pretty fast Utah, even for a human male. She seems confused by your questions. She says, "I'm so sorry about my butthole boyfriend."

UTAH: "It's okay, everyone has one," I say, "And you mean, Man Friend, I am sure." McAdams, guard that door, k?

SPENCER: I'm on it. Rolled a 3 though.

LM: You're barely holding it shut now. Dea jay Lazlo and company are saying something about a "doosh bag." He'll be in soon. Sheesh, you all haven't even made it out of the bar yet.

SPENCER: So a bag of dooshes in our world. Hmm. Wonder what dooshes are. Sorry about the door team. Athletics is not my area of expertise. We've only got a couple of rounds, at most.

KAITLYN: We're not in debate though, right?

LM: Not at the moment.

SPENCER: Then, I'm going to use my hipster modern clothing skill to identify the jacket. Someone might help get some information out of this female.

LM: Congrats, It's logical. Very high-powered. Strong dweomer of fashion. Past your ability to detect fully though.

SPENCER: I'm putting it on. Might help us. It's so fun to wear clothes right Utah?

LM: You put it on?

SPENCER: Yes!

LM: You put on the jacket?

SPENCER: Yes!

KAITLYN, UTAH: No!

LM: Well, congrats. It's cursed. Your societal presence modifier is going to be a palm tree in a hurricane.

SPENCER: What does that mean in the real world?

LM: You'll see.

KAITLYN: Pickles!! We've got to stick to plans here. From now on, no jumping over bars or trying logical items until we know what they do? Agreed?

SPENCER: Also, no sniffing any more crotches in Sandy Go until we sort out what is going on with people and buttholes.

UTAH: Good idea. Okay, I'll get right to the point, "Good day, Lady Selena. My name is Utah Spicolli. I saw the runes upon your skin reading "a key poppy" and received your wink gesture, so I rushed in to assist you. I am a surfer as you can tell by this prodigious 6 foot 8 inch surfboard here. This is my legal comrade Kaitlyn and our craft brewing trusty bearded human, Spencer McAdams. We are at your service."

KAITLYN: I wink.

SPENCER: I'm actually gonna try a blink this time. That's both eyes right?

LM: Ouch, it doesn't go too well with the blink. Your newly donned cursed jacket is giving you a -4 to opposite sex attraction. She clearly rebukes you as a

potential breeding partner. You do get the sense that you'd be really great at a yo mama joke battle though. Should you wish to pursue that.

SPENCER: Doubt that would help. Lazlo is practically pounding down the door by the way here, friends. I can't hold him much longer.

LM: "My boyfriend is a total butthole stalker. I can't believe how you all handled him. How *you* handled him, Spicolli.

UTAH: Told you she'd find me attractive! I wink at her again. Then, I ask why Lazlo stalks her butthole.

LM: Selena doesn't answer. But she takes off her bar apron, and she hangs it on a hook next to the sign about stupid people. She says, "I swear, I've been looking for one decent reason to quit before those lawyers shut this place down and this shit show is just the reason."

KAITLYN: "Would you like company to the shit show? I…I saw the sign."

LM: Uh oh, just then, the lock at the door is busted, and the door swings in. Dea jay Lazlo is standing there in his beer-stained tank top, and golden *bling*. His mouth is open, and his arms are crossed. His minions flank him. His face is very expressive right now. "You trying to make a move on my girl, crotch-sniffer?" he says. To make matters far worse, the music behind him in the bar just became much

louder. You can feel his dea jay energy radiating off his beer-stained body. Lazlo now has lair actions, people. And you're trapped!

KAITLYN: I was just about to get invited to a shit show! Okay. Attention humans. I step forward. I flap my—

LM: You don't have—

KAITLYN: Right. Ok. I step forward. I flap my *arms*.

UTAH/SPENCER: Here we go.

KAITLYN: "According to human penis code 287.19 you are in violation of direct assault of this human male's right to verbal disagreement."

SPENCER: What are you doing? How do you know there's a penis code?

KAITLYN: I read there's a penis everything in human culture. Stalling and bluffing. Watch me work my reality, people!

LM: Your bluff works to confuse the dea jay for 2 rounds. Congrats, and good use of your legal apprenticeship feat.

SPENCER: While Jacoby is stalling, I'm using my first level hipster ability to identify the ingredients on the food preparation tables.

LM: It's *avaca dough*.

SPENCER: Sweet nectar! This is green gold. I'll create a spread from that avaca dough. Mixed with lightly toasted bread, I can create a consumable product that turns any social class of level 4 or lower. Turned victims must eat all of the toast, wipe their lips daintily with a single napkin, and moan for 3 rounds.

LM: There's heating equipment and bread on the work table near you. Your ritual has begun. Well done. While Kaitlyn stalls, you've created a quick avaca dough spread and applied it to toasted bread. It is virtually irresistible to human beings. Dea jay Lazlo is clearly smelling it. He's stunned now, and better news, both of his sidekicks are too. They were actually hipsters in level one dea jay disguise so they had disadvantage to spreads and dips.

UTAH: Wow.

SPENCER: Yeah, I'm telling you the hipster class is—

LM: Uh oh, dea jay Lazlo was just empowered by the music behind him, and he's been given a lair reset role. He is choosing a dea jay lair action that is unfortunately for you an immediate reaction. He takes a bite of the avaca dough toast, wipes the green goop off his face with the back of his human hand, and stares directly at McAdams. "Nice avaca dough toast," says the dea jay. "But it could use a bit more pepper, don't you think?"

UTAH: Oh pickles! That's a human czar chasm, right?

LM: Yep. And you all better just be thankful that he doesn't have his *mike* on him right now. McAdams, I'm going to need both a social *and* an emotional roll from you.

SPENCER: Eight and four.

LM: Fail and fail! You've just been *czar chasmed* about your avaca dough toast. You must know that the hipster class is extremely vulnerable to this attack. You have taken 6 points of social damage and 5 points of emotional damage. That's 11 total social *and* emotional damage. You have only 1 point of each left.

UTAH: What happens at zero?

LM: Depends on class. For hipsters, any type, you'll lose all hipster abilities, will begin either *jernaling* or sharing your feelings with other hipsters. It can lead to a *nervous breakdown*, which is like being stunned indefinitely to a hipster, if you do not find *social media* quickly.

KAITLYN: What's social media?

LM: We'll get to it when or if we get there. Dea jay Lazlo puts down the avaca dough toast, and smiles his human smile. He points to Selena and says, "Look *babe*, I got some business to take care of, but I'll see you later on. As for these losers, boys!" Then he snaps his fingers. Behind him, the two followers step

forward. "Bring me my jacket. I've got more important shit to deal with tonight."

KAITLYN: I step forward. "First, she's a grown woman, not a baby. Secondly, there's no shit more important than the shit in this shit show!"

UTAH: Are you crazy? This is a physical debate now Kaitlyn. You are intelligence based, remember?

KAITLYN: "And your music *sucks*!"

SPENCER: Oh, my sweet buttercup dew.

LM: Lazlo's mouth is hanging open.

KAITLYN: Trust me. I know what I'm doing. I look the dea jay right in both of his eyes and I say in Eng Lish, "You know Lazlo, you look familiar! As an associate legal analyst for the law firm of Stintz and Stetsons, by chance has someone here recently gotten into a little legal trouble in our not-too-distant past?"

UTAH: What the swamp are you doing Jacoby?

LM: The dea jay continues to stare at you with his two eyes. He fingers his bling necklace. Then, he holds up a hand and forms it into a fist. His minions stop next to him. He seems to be considering your bluff. Your stall has worked Jacoby.

KAITLYN: It did?

UTAH: Really?

KAITLYN: Now, at this very moment, I kick open the side door to where the breeze is blowing, and in hurls a furry ball of fury. You hear, *"MEEEEEOOOOW!!!!!!!!!!!"*

SPENCER: You set this up with the LM!

LM: She sure did! And just then an orange and white striped blur of madness hurtles through the crack in the door. Meyers the cat comes streaking in to the bar and to your aid Kaitlyn Jacoby! Meyers first flies across the tile floor, lunges up and attaches himself to dea jay Lazlo's face. He is now blind and swirling in a circle. He has lost lair actions and his leadership modifier drops to zero. As a result, his minions are temporarily stunned. You've got two rounds.

UTAH: Well done Kailyn Esquire! I grab Selena with one hand and my surfboard with the other one and without a tail whipping behind me, or hopping on hooves, I rush out of the door with my two feet.

SPENCER: I grab some avaca dough toast and rush out behind them! Can I roll though to see if he was bluffing about the pepper?

KAITLYN: "Come on, Meyers!"

LM: "Meeeeeeooooowwwww!!!!!!!!!"

Chapter 4

A First Kiss of the Humankind

LM: Congratulations, you all have survived your first encounter with a dea jay! I haven't calculated your reality points yet, but they're not small.

UTAH: Level 2?

LM: Dream on' little human. Now, where was I...oh here we go. The night is filled with the sounds of musical instruments and humans singing, yelling, hooting, clapping, stomping, and talking incessantly and at high volume. The air outside the bar is warm and most people are wearing bright colors and carrying green, white, and red striped banners. In the center of the banner, there is a picture of a giant roc holding a baby dragon tenderly in it's mother's loving clutches.

KAITLYN: Oh, whittle baby.

SPENCER: Baby drakes are so cute!

LM: A large group of brightly plumed people march by. Welcome to Sinkody Miyo! As you spill out of the Tiki Mermaid, you realize that you've entered a realistic world of human motion and human sound. All around you people are singing and dancing. Like colorful jungle birds in flight, a parade of humans stroll by on their long legs. Some bang well-manufactured drums, others are shaking *maracas*, a kind of rattle that looks as though it was snatched off the end of a wyvern's tail. Dozens of other humans line the street on both sides while a river of colorful humanity streams down the wide paved trails known as streets. Many of the humans are wearing wide-brimmed hats called some *braros*. Nearly all are holding sweet smelling alcoholic drinks called *mahr-gritas* which they keep in *plassed-tick* cups. Over the din of this crowd, you can only faintly hear dea jay Lazlo cursing you from behind.

UTAH: Ok people. We've got to get Selena away from the dea jay, not to mention ourselves! This human parade is a perfect opportunity.

UTAH: I am going to attempt to "borrow" some braros and I'll walk into the parade.

LM: Sure. Just give me a roll for both human swag and successful dance rhythm.

KAITLYN: I'll do the same.

SPENCER: Me too. But instead of some braros, I'm going to try and snatch a pair of maracas-one for each hand with disposable thumbs!

LM: Based on your rolls. Here's what happens, *amigos*. Spicolli, you still got hold of Selenas' hand and it just so happens she is from the human tribe that invented Sinkody Miyo. She gives you a whopping +5 for both braro fashion and human dancing and you've successfully blended right into the crowd, following her rhythm.

UTAH: Look at me friends! I've never even danced with toes before!

LM: Doesn't matter. Dance moves in the real world are a universal language. Plus, your attraction modifier has risen with the possibility of being a potential breeding match to Selena.

UTAH: Sweet honey nectar!

LM: You McAdams get to use your daily swag ability. You put some of the braros on wrong but since you're a hipster somehow it works.

SPENCER: Weird.

LM: Right? You unfortunately though do stand out because human dancing does not look like a rabid squirrel with his back legs stuck in a hunter's trap.

SPENCER: It was worth a try. Dancing here on two leg—

LM: But! Just when you think you'll be spotted by the dea jay, who is right at this moment scanning the parade, Jacoby over here saves the day yet again.

KAITLYN: I do? I mean, I do! How do I do it this time?

LM: Well, it isn't you so much as your maracas! The musical instruments of *Mecks Icko* enhance your swag and your dance moves. Not to mention nothing makes a path through a swarm of moving legs like a cat familiar. Following Meyers orange and white tail through the crowd you navigate right into the heart of the turbulent paraders. Your musical instrument also gives McAdams a +2 to rhythm and just when one of Lazlo's henchmen are about to spot him- POOF! You all camouflage!

UTAH: Humans can camouflage? What!

LM: The Sinkody Miyo celebration is a tempest of energy, sound and human happiness. The Mecks Icko tribe really knows how to do festivals. Soon, you've rounded a corner. When you are out of sight from scrying eyes, you move out of the parade, and onto the street curb. Utah, Selena comes to stand before

you on the curb so that her eyes align perfectly with yours. Lights from poles above you cascade down over you both, illuminating her human symmetry like a nymph in starlight. She smooths back her hair with her two hands, grabs your arms and closes her two eyes. Her lips begin to puff out.

UTAH: Is she having an allergic reaction!? Did a giant centipede bite her lips?

LM: No.

UTAH: What are her ears doing? Are they up, back, sideways?

LM: Human ears don't do any of that.

UTAH: Right. Well, then what should I do?!

KAITLYN: You troglodyte. This is a human ritual. She wants you to do something called *kissing*. I read all about it in the Man Manual.

UTAH: Oh wow! Already? Well yeah. Can I have a minute to study the guidebook here?

KAITLYN: Chapter 69.

UTAH: Thanks.

LM: No. You may not study the guide book.

UTAH: Ok. Well, then I lean in, extend my teeth and—

KAITLYN: No! Just use your lips. Can I give him a +2 if I assist with kissing Selena?

LM: No. And you can't metagame this together. The guidebook is very specific about this being a solo action between two willing participants. No interference!

UTAH: Fine. I'll kiss alone. If I fail, save yourselves.

KAITLYNL Well, I don't feel like this is helping out the kiss, so I do want to yell at Spicolli Kiss Giver, "Don't use your teeth!"

UTAH: "No teeth? Then I go in nose first. *Right* between her lips."

LM: Selena's lips tighten around your nose. Then, like a sword in a scabbard, the lips give away allowing your nose to slide right into her mouth. You feel an odd sense of warmth and moisture especially around your nostrils.

UTAH: Wow. I'm experiencing a real human kiss…

LM: Yeah, the guidebook says that you'll be in a sense of "ecstasy" like when a green slime finds a body at the bottom of a bog and doesn't surface for an age.

UTAH: Wow.

LM: Selena's lips now move slowly downward to your own two lips. And this is the moment when you feel a strong aura of human attunement for Selena. Congratulations Utah, you have initiated and successfully conducted your first kiss of the humankind. Your attraction modifier just permanently rose by 2!

UTAH: Snowflakes in spring time!

SPENCER: Well done, lover boy.

UTAH: So are Selena and I now married?

LM: No.

UTAH: Will either of us bear offspring at equinox?

LM: Whoa! That's nowhere near a guarantee yet. This is only phase one in a human courtship.

UTAH: Phase two is…?

SPENCER: I believe it's called Base 2. Read an article on courtship roleplay encounters in Librarian Scroll last week. Great issue by the way.

LM: We'll get to that. First, Selena opens her eyes. She had them closed the whole time for some reason you don't fully understand. She says, "Utah, I like you. You aren't like the other guys I've dated before. Your friends are….sorta cool too." Then she looks at

McAdams and Jacoby. "Will you all walk me home? I feel safe, somehow with you…people"

SPENCER: "No problem," I say. *She called us people!*

UTAH: "We'll do it for three dollars. The type that folds if you don't mind, Selena." Then, I wink.

KAITLYN: Ask her for five! But you know, we'll take four.

LM: Selena seems confused at first as if your request is not appropriate in this situation. She rummages in her satchel anyway though.

KAITLYN: You mean *purse*.

LM: Right. She rummages in her purse and pulls out a folding money bill. It's green and white with a number five on it. There's a picture of a strange human in the middle. She hands it to you, Utah.

UTAH: Bulls eyes!

LM: Selena leans in and kisses Utah one last time with her puffy lips, this time on your cheek. She says, "Keep the change, handsome."

UTAH: Huh? I'm rolling perception on that one. How do I keep change from happening?

LM: You've got no idea what she's talking about. But you watch her walk away, through a crowd of party goers, into an alley, where humans keep entrances to

their domiciles. Before disappearing into one, she turns back to Utah, "I hope I see you again, Utah." Then she says goodbye to McAdams and to Jacoby, bends down and drags a hand along Meyers back and tail.

UTAH: I tell her not to worry because there's now a pheromone trail so I can stalk her whenever I need. In fact, I'd like to tell her that I'll be a far better stalker than her other guy, the dea jay Lazlo. So she can rest well with that knowledge tonight.

LM: Too late. She is gone, and her domicile door is closed.

UTAH: Well, that was fun, hey kids?

KAITLYN: Yeah, and we've got five folding dollars to spend. Not bad for a kiss and a walk!

SPENCER: We should find a logical item shop! I've been reading about Marry Cans. They are incredible tinkerers and craftsman; they have all kinds of logical items in big cities like this, supposedly on every corner. At least that's what it says in Humans and History.

UTAH: Ok, well let's find a corner then. I walk down the street with my dance movements going in both legs and I'm looking for a corner. What am I seeing?

LM: The corner nearest you is actually brightly lit by lick trissity.

KAITLYN, UTAH, SPENCER: That's what the bugbear—

LM: Stop it. The entire edifice seems to be constructed of glass. Inside are shelves, boxes and containers overfilling with bottles, bags, and packages of brightly colored labels. It's a treasure trove inside, but one which you'll have to pay human money for—or risk being *poh-leeced*. One lone human shopkeeper is leaning over a counter near to the entrance behind many colorful packages for sale. There is a large sign over the entrance in bright green lick trissity.

KAITLYN: Can I read it?

LM: You all can. These aren't letters, they are numbers. The sign reads, "7-11"

SPENCER: Oh I get it. Everything in there is going to cost between seven and eleven of these folding papers.

LM: Maybe.

UTAH: But we don't have enough of them yet.

KAITLYN: Hey McAdams. Have you searched that jacket properly? Didn't I read somewhere that humans have pouches in all their clothes that they like to put stuff like money in?

LM: Pockets.

KAITLYN: Yeah, those! What's in your…how do you say more than one pocket?

LM: Pocketsesss.

UTAH: Yeah then, what's in your *pocketsessss*?

SPENCER: Wait. Spicolli's onto something. There's something in here.

UTAH: Does it fold?

SPENCER: I think so, yeah.

KAITLYN: Well, whip it out!

Law Firm of Minick and Minick

9650 Tourmaline Road Suite 104

La Jolla, CA 91201

Lazlo, If she won't sign tonight then you know what to do. Remember, we aren't the only ones interested

in Matilda's property so handle this with extreme discretion. It's essential that you secure the property tonight. We'll return from holiday ourselves Tuesday. You can bring the file to us then. 9 o'clock pm. Sharp.

Don't let us down Lazlo. We're counting on <u>you</u>. If you ever want to see that record label, then your career is counting on <u>us</u> too.

M & M

UTAH: Wow, what a clue! It all makes sense now. This is why Matilda was behaving so strangely at the Tiki Mermaid. She just flapped her bar away to a pair of devel-lopers! This is why Lazlo was there. He's probably been charming Selena, seducing her with his high masculinity modifier and rapping ability, in order to gain her trust. Probably to gain information, and to set the whole thing in motion. Poor Selena. No one deserves to be seduced in a rap song.

SPENCER: Well now we know. This is big time. To think we're going to be up against two, not one, but two greater real estate devel-lopers. Wow. These sons of a basilisk aren't just some minor side quest. Are they?

LM: Not saying anything.

UTAH: This is the whole adventure, right here. We're talking about *bankruptcy*, *repossessions*, *eviction*, not to mention the fact that every time these villains play *golf*, they gain 1d4+3 more henchmen!

SPENCER: What's golf?

UTAH: No idea. But that doesn't matter. What does matter is that this enemy can attack us in nearly every single way that we can't defend ourselves in yet. Jacoby, what do you make of this letter? Is any of this even logical?

KAITLYN: Well, it's not good. This is what real estate devel-lopers do. They get you with what looks like logic tricks. But the weird part is that this letter isn't logic. It's illogical. The way devel-lopers operate is that they have so many resources and so many lair powers that when they hit you from multiple ranges, you can't defend against anything properly. Devel-lopers use a terrible item called a *file*. Whatever they put in that file, once it is opened after a sinister ritual, *will* come true. Worse, in this letter, we have additional corruption logic. Clearly, these devel-lopers are using their twin developer ability to corrupt city officials into a quiet land grab.

SPENCER: How do you grab land?

KAITLYN: Exactly as it sounds but instead of using their hands they do it by putting human dwellings on the land instead.

SPENCER: That sounds like marking one's favorite tree stump in the meadow down by the—

KAITLYN: But there's more. These so-called M&Ms are probably attempting to manipulate Matilda into believing she has no defenses. Basically, they use a type of illogic called 'gaslighting.' I only just recently heard about it from a gargoyle friend playing a CEO. No doubt, Matilda signing that paper was to her, her last chance to walk away with anything from her bar and not be completely bank-ruptured. And the bad news is that these are very high-level powers we are talking about. These devel-lopers have probably made Lah Hoya their lair for generations. We're talking about a very dreadful set of villains here.

SPENCER: I thought this adventure was for levels 1-3 by the way.

UTAH: Great. So now we've got greater real estate devel-lopers after us since whoever these M&Ms are will know we took Lazlo's letter. This letter gives us a clue, but it also puts a target on our backs. What I'm trying to say is that while this letter is in our hands, their M&M hatred is going to be burning for us in other places.

SPENCER: I think I understand you. Do you mean that the M &M s will be salivating for us in their mouths, but this letter isn't doing that in our hands?

UTAH: Precisely! And that is why we have the upper tail! Don't you see my human friends? We know where their lair is. We know what they want. We know about their sinister file. Their file of...

KAITLYN: File of...

SPENCER: File of...

UTAH: Dread!

SPENCER, KAITLYN, LM: Yeah!

UTAH: We know who their henchmen are. They may know who we are, but they don't know anything else about us, and the sooner we confront them, the less they'll know!

SPENCER: Uh oh. This is exactly how we got rank ruptured in Warriors of Wall Street.

KAITLYN: Be irrational Spicolli! We have one cursed logical item. We can't afford to buy more at this seven-to-eleven shop. We're still level one, McAdams here is in social and emotional shock. We're all nearly bankruptured except for a small fee you collected from Selena.

SPENCER: Jacoby is right. We mess with this file and we are doomed. How are we even going to sleep and regain any powers with this festival going on? If we somehow do gain new powers by leveling up, we couldn't use them. I'm still a level one hipster for swamp sakes. I can't even detect organic produce yet! I'm all out of daily garlic cloves.

UTAH: For the love and pride of the faerie folk, keep your horn on straight McAdams. Look. We take this one hydra head at a time. Let's see if we can at least mini-quest for the proprietor of this seven-to-eleven establishment. We've still got two days before the file opens. We'll keep our ears up and our tails balanced, earn some reality points the human way and score some gear in the process. When we're ready we'll find a way to take the battle to the devel-lopers. With a little pixie dust, we can get to the law firm before Lazlo's meeting on Thors Day. When those devel-lopers arrive, we can be waiting for them. Kaitlyn can sabotage their loopholes, I can surf any webs they've spun and you McAdams, when we get you back to full social *and* emotional fulfillment, you can hit them with your best organics.

SPENCER: Hopefully by then I can make a platter of charcuterie that even a devel-loper can't resist.

KAITLYN: Now there's the prancer in the moonbeams I know!

UTAH: And we'll high tail it back to Matilda's, give her the good news, count our reality points and leave this adventure like the level three heroes we know we can be!

KAITLYN: Maybe you'll even make second phase with Selena.

SPENCER: We have done stupider things. Even in our world.

KAITLYN: Remember that time you pulled on both eye stalks of that—

UTAH: Of course, we have! Now human game faces on. This place looks loaded with everything we need. Let's play it cold and see if we can get this human doing what humans do best.

KAITLYN: Eating?

SPENCER: Staring at hand-held devices?

LM: Good guesses. You landed at two and three respectively. But the latest guidebook says number one is *talking*.

Chapter 5

Potions of Monster Energy and a Hoop of Hill Giant Hula

LM: You pull the handle to the curio shop, and you enter what can only be described as an enormous glistening treasure vault. Your weak human eyes fill instantly with kingly, shining treasure of every conceivable variety. Even your sad, puny human noses are also quite happy. Aromas of rich, savory, and sweet delicacies which line shelf after shelf waft into your human nose. Considering that humans can walk around all day and not experience nose-joy, you are in a state of meadow.

Spencer: Woot!

Utah: There ain't nothing like *real* human food!

LM: The chamber you now stand in is brightly lit by lick trissity from long lanterns that hang from above. There are rows and rows of what appear to be logical items of every shape and size in boxes, bags, and glass potion containers. Behind massive sets of glass doors on the north wall lies more rows of potion bottles with various runes and labels plastered over each item. Behind the window some kind of air elemental stirs, creating a fog upon the window. For some reason, the elemental is keeping these potions cold. No doubt the humans use lick trissity to feed the elemental's power. There is a row of strange scrolls opened on display in racks along the windows near the entrance you now stand in front of. To your right is a counter as high as a cockatrice's top feather. Many more logical items of a smaller variety litter the surface of the counter and seem to be kept safe in small display boxes. Behind the counter sits a human male with so much facial hair you can only see his squinty brown eyes and pink nose.

Kaitlyn: Finally, a human that makes some sense.

LM: He also has very long curly hair sticking out of his head above the face too, and he is wearing a sort of blue smock, like a blacksmith's apron. His name tag says "Bart."

Spencer: What's he doing?

LM: Right now he seems fairly absorbed in a scroll that he's laid out on the counter. When you enter, he says, "Ohlameegos. Happy Sinkody Miyo. We're running low on provisions. Just that last case left." He points a finger at a box about the size of a pond turtle resting on the chamber floor behind you. "Let me know if y'all got any questions, k?" He then returns to his studying.

Kaitlyn: Logic-user. They have to constantly study.

Utah: I say, "Cool, bro." Then, nonchalantly I begin to scan the items behind me.

LM: Bart sort of nods as if he expected you to do this. He seems impressed with your use of the term "bro."

Utah: It's a surfer thing. You can use bro or dude interchangeably with other human names provided that the intended recipient of the dude or bro is aware that you are a surfer or skater class.

Spencer: That's cool.

Utah: Right?

LM: Well, nicely done indeed Utah. You can all look around the shop a little if you want. Just let me know what you want to investigate and we'll see what you discover.

Utah: I'm going to check out the potion bottles.

Spencer: I'm looking for curse removals, obviously. Also, any hipster components that are both organic and not in a can or aluminum tin.

Kaitlyn: That's redundant. Hipster components lose their logic, essentially they become ineffective once placed in a can or tin.

Spencer: Makes sense.

Utah: Ok. Well, I'm going to look for items that can help us in another altercation. You know. Something to boost my social and emotional modifiers or at least cause a ruckus.

Kaitlyn: What's a ruckus?

Utah: Not sure. But the Man Manual said it can be a lot of fun. How's our search going?

LM: In a fern frond, some of you rolled well and some of you did not. But here's what you find. Spicolli, when you open those cold glass doors on the north wall, you are stunned by frigid air and have a -2 to physical reactions for three rounds.

Utah: It was trapped?

LM: Not on purpose. Inside, you find several potions of something called 'monster energy'.

Spencer: Makes sense humans would make something like that. Aren't they afraid of us?

LM: Some of you, maybe. But your kin? Don't make me laugh! Now, you also identify another as a potion of dew from the mountains.

Utah: They drink mountain's dew too? Potion of monster energy, dew from the mountains. Wow. What will I find next? A magical sword?

LM: Funny you should ask. There's actually an intriguing red box on a shelf that draws your attention to it. It's dusty and looks as though it's been resting there for quite some time. On the top of the box is a picture of a colossal red dragon guarding her treasure. An interloping human on a horse is bothering her.

Utah: Sounds about right. Any runes?

LM: Yes, It appears as though this box contains a game. It's called "Dungeons and Dragons, The Role-Playing Game."

Kaitlyn: You did that on purpose.

LM: Haha, yeah well wouldn't it be hilarious if these humans had a game like Law Firms and Librarians?

Utah: Come on dude. That's squirrel nut-hoarding crazy. Even for your imagination. Anything else here in the real world?

LM: Yes. In a corridor of goods and wares displayed in the center of the shop, Kailyn has found a box of rings on display!

Spencer: RINGS!!!!

Kaitlyn: Wow! This place is a trove. What kind of ring is it?

LM: You've got no idea. But it's in a clear package and the gem on the ring is massive. Looks like a brilliantly cut ruby. About the size of a bumble bee.

Utah: Out of our price range…

Kaitlyn: Rings are always important.

Utah: And often cursed.

Kaitlyn: Never pass up a ring.

LM: And finally, there's a small stone-like object which is wrapped in clear plassed tick. Attached to it is a paper sign in Eng Lish. You have a really hard time reading it, but when you smell it, you notice it has a very strong odor.

Kaitlyn: What does it smell like?

LM: Ass. Slight hint of feces.

Kaitlyn: So, I found a turd?

Utah: Maybe a lost dingleberry? Perhaps we can return it for a reward!

LM: Perhaps and no. But there's something special about this turd.

Kaitlyn: Well, there is something special about every turd really.

Spencer: What about me? Am I finding anything?

LM: Oh, you found some great stuff yourself. You decided to walk around the back of the store, and you discovered a box filled with what looks like tall and spongy hollow pond reeds. Sort of like large noodles. Next to that was another box containing what looks like spongy shields. Above that, on a shelf is a collection of goggles, like dwarves wear deep in their mines-only smaller.

Spencer: Oh, I try them on.

Utah: Don't try them on!

Kaitlyn: Try them on!

LM: You put them on.

Spencer: And?

LM: You actually do not notice any benefit in your sad human vision. If anything, now your vision is slightly more blurred. Whatever purpose they serve seems not to be immediately clear.

Spencer: Hmmm? Lame as a horse I'd say. I wonder what they do. I can't identify them until we take a long rest.

Kaitlyn: Yeah. I can't either.

LM: There's also one last thing you notice that seems of interest. It's a giant belt, resting in a crate by the noodle.

Spencer: Like a gauntlet?

LM: Well...this one is a bit different. It seems to be meant for a hill giant, or maybe a very large ogre I suppose.

Spencer: What is going on here? I thought this was a shop for humans in the real world?

LM: This belt is made of that human material we discussed called plassed tick.

SPENCER: What if it's a storm giant's ring instead?

UTAH: It doesn't matter which breed of giant it's for. How's it going to help us in the real world?

LM: Hey. I'm just giving you the information here. I will provide you this small hint: That two average sized humans could fit inside of it. Or one really big one I suppose. Been a while since I have seen a human of course so—

KAITLYN: But why would a human do that?

77

UTAH: To trap them?

LM: You aren't sure. Alright, McAdams. I got some great news for you. You found some items with information in Eng Lish runes right on their packages.

SPENCER: I did?

LM: Yeah! First, you pick up what at first appears to be a human tin. This type of thing ordinarily has very tantalizing food inside of it. But upon closer inspection of the runes that wrap around it, you realize inside is housed a variety of snakes which will spring out to enormous sizes when the top is opened.

SPENCER: Magical snakes? What kind of reality world is this? There's a magical sword in there too right?

UTAH: Right?

LM: No. The snakes are not real. It's a cleverly designed logical item using metallic springs. The snakes function *logically* as a powerful illusion with a potent two round stunning effect, radius 6 feet on can's center.

SPENCER: So...it's a can of fake snakes, got it. Could be useful I suppose. Anything else?

LM: Next to this can of snakes is a skinnier can with a red top. An image is drawn on the side of a very happy human child. He is smiling profusely and

pushing down a red button on the top of a can just like the one you are holding.

SPENCER: I will now remove the cap from the can and use one of my two disposable thumbs to do the exact same thing to the can as this human child.

LM: Instantaneously red webbing flies out of a small hole in the nozzle, coating the items on the shelf in red slippery coiling strands.

SPENCER: I drop the can and hunch down into an attack stance!

KAITLYN: I do the exact same and shout, "Your day has come, villains!"

LM: You hear Bart yell from the front of the store, "Hey! What in the hell are you lot up to back there? You guys better not be playfighting with the pool noodles dude."

KAITLYN: Pickles!

UTAH: Playfighting, as if we weren't serious heroes around—

SPENCER: Oh, I get it, the webs are like the snakes too, right. They are meant to look real, but they are fake-real?

KAITLYN: What is it with humans and cute pets which are fake-real?

LM: Humans don't like snakes. They feel the same way about spiders.

UTAH: And sharks. Says so in the Surfer's Background.

Kaitlyn: I wonder if the rumors are true and they really wouldn't like us all that—

LM: Interesting, but while you all are deliberating which of you the humans would like least, you hear a bell chime. The same as the one that rang when you walked into the shop. Bart's voice welcomes some mysterious merchant or merchants beyond your vision, "Can I help you girls?" Answering Bart, you now hear a female human's voice in a strange dialect of Eng Lish that none of you can fully understand. I'm using your passive perceptions to give you a chance to collect some of it at least. It's very high-pitched at times. Other times it sounds extremely long-winded as though it takes the speaker a very long time to finish a single word. The reply sounds a little like this, "Liiiiiike yahhhh hairy man. We like need some friiickin alc-hall to keep this party goin'. Comprendy?" Then, there's another voice speaking in the same dialect. "Like can you help us by giving a dough nation of some frickin' beers to me and my sorrrrrity sisters? We've got sissers waiting for us from five different srrrrroooorties. You'll be a damn Theta, Zeta, Gamma hero to the houses up the street." This is followed by a lot of high-pitched laughing, and giggling.

SPENCER: What's giggling?

LM: It's like laughing only picture that a jungle parrot is doing it while diseased with a debilitating condition that makes it shake all over.

SPENCER: Got it. Sounds painful. Poor humans.

LM: Bart answers the mysterious merchant in normal Eng Lish. "Sorry girls. I wish I could help out. But the owner would have my head on a platter if I screwed up inventory on Sinkody Miyo." This is followed by terrible female wailing.

SPENCER: As in they turned into banshees?

KAITLYN: Harpies?

UTAH: People! This is it. Our first step towards solving the File of Dread. We can do two things at the same time. First, we help Bart save his head from being served on a platter. Meanwhile we help change these sisters back to normal from their harpy giggles, and we're on our way. We'll be rewarded, can furnish ourselves with all the logical gear we can carry from this fine establishment, and take the battle right to the devellopers themselves. I prepare for debate, goodly Library Master!

KAITYLN: Okay, I'm in. Preparing for debate.

SPENCER: Me too. Debate engaged!

KAITLYN: What's the plan Utah?

UTAH: Well, I haven't exactly got one of those yet…

SPENCER: Utah!

KAITLYN: Spicolli!

Chapter 6

The Battle of the Five Sror-Tee Sisters

SPENCER: I'm getting into this stampede early. I step out on my non-hooved feet, which should grip the material the floor is made of better than a hoof, correct?

LM: Correct.

SPENCER: Excellent, then I step out from behind the edible goods and logical wares around me. I clear my throat, pull back my lips and speak Eng Lish: "Excuse me, human ladies," I tell them, "I am a hipster with a background in brew-making. I believe I may be of some assistance here."

KAITLYN: Remember. They are using their high sexual attraction modifiers to score free beer from this male human, Bart. And now you're going to get hit with any area effects and most likely be forced to give them free things too since you are vulnerable to such an attack. Look you horned grass-eater, you're within their 10 foot radius!

SPENCER: I. Can't. Help. It. It's. The. Jacket's. Curse.

LM: He isn't lying. Cursed jacket, remember?

UTAH: I think it's more you.

LM: Bart is staring at you now Spencer. And when you step out, you see the people that belong to the high-pitched wailing voices. They are indeed all females. You count five of them. Each is wearing their hair in a horse's tail as though their heads were a horse's ass. I am sure you find this quite entertaining.

SPENCER: I do.

LM: They each stand with the bulk of their weight on one hip as opposed to equally dispersed weight between both hips. All of them have their mouths wide open.

SPENCER: I drop into a pre-lunge crouch!

LM: I don't think you understand. This is not a physical attack behavior but instead a display of

territorial defense. This type of human stands with weight on only one hip in malls, school corridors, and during all festivals where loud music is played. Humans of any kind keep their mouths open at different times for many reasons, the most logical one in this situation is that they are surprised.

SPENCER: But why are they wearing their hair as if their heads were a horse's ass?

LM: It's typical of female *Merry Cans* of this bracket of age and social status. For *sror-tee* sisters it's very normal.

KAITLYN: An actual *sror-tee* coven. Oh. Mah. Gawd!

LM: Well done Jacoby. You are not sure what they must have looked like before the giggling and cackling began, but you are seeing this coven of five in all their glory. They currently appear to be much less clothed than normal humans. All of them are wearing very flimsy and/or ripped garments around their chest area, and short pants which humans just call *shorts*. Much of their skin is showing, various shades of human skin tones. All have very high attraction modifiers, so Spencer you are finding it difficult to concentrate on other parts of the scene.

SPENCER: Kissable?

LM: Highly. But not in their current condition. The cackling noises they make negate any male breeding desires in a 3' foot radius, even as they attract males

into the zone with high sexual attraction. It's a sort of breeding trap, although there is still not very much known about the origin of this behavior. But I'm just telling you what you all know from the guide books.

SPENCER: I feel like these girls need our help. That's not the jacket talking. That's me now.

KAITLYN: Riiiiiiight.

LM: Bart fails his persuasion skill check. Sorry McAdams, you need to roll too, and at disadvantage because of the anti-swag due to your jacket. And blame McAdams here for putting the jacket on, but don't blame him for stepping out. The jacket's swag level forces him to involve himself when tobacco or other inhaled herbs are involved. He also has disadvantage because of the sror-tee sisters giggling.

LM: And since he's a hipster subclass, the twin effects of the jacket and his gender are only made worse when it's a beer-related incident. He has no choice but to respond here-that is until it's removed of course.

SPENCER: Fat chance of that happening any time soon.

LM: Uh oh humans. Just then the bell chimes again. Four young male humans enter wearing shades over their eyes despite the late hour. They are all quite skinny, and runes appear on their skin, like Selena had only larger and in more swirly script. Each is also wearing minimal garments around the chest

area. You can see just the smallest of budding muscles ripple like teeny tiny pond waves across their chest. But below the waist, they must be carrying a very heavy load because their pants are sagging to the point they are nearly falling off of their hips.

SPENCER: In the front or the back?

LM: The back, mostly. And remember, Utah and Kaitlyn can't see any of this yet.

SPENCER: That's a shame about their sag. Must reduce their speed quite a bit. What's in the sag? Dingleberries?

LM: You aren't sure. And yes, humans will do a lot for fashion, and to increase their attraction or prowess modifier. Surely, you've noticed already. In human society that stuff is a real trade-off. Play one of these fellas sometime and you'll find out.

LM: The most saggy and scripted of the lot, who is clearly the lead human, sticks out his chin like a sort of featherless parrot, on the highest branch of a tree. He calls out to Bart, "Sup homeboy! We back for some more poison."

SPENCER: More dea jays? I'm rolling perception and investigation just in case.

LM: No, not dea jays. What we've got here friends is a brand-new subclass of the human lurker variety. This particular subclass uses intimidation, social status and group tactics to achieve it's goals. Like dea

jays, they carry bling, mostly around the neck, but it is less pronounced. They most commonly wear sunglasses, day or night, as it helps with their intimidation tactics. Also, their dialect is very unique, and those who speak it within a certain area of effect gain several advantages. As we've already discussed, they also *sag*.

KAITLYN: I read that you can often tell their level based on the amount of sag. So, McAdams, keep your two eyes open for that.

SPENCER: That's nice but what do we call them?

LM: Well, a single member of the tribe is called a *homeboy*. More than one, and they might be called *gang members*, whether they are or not. It's sort of complicated in human society because humans have a hard time distinguishing patterns in each other's behavior versus their outward appearance.

UTAH: Humans are weird. I am telling you.

LM: But if they appear in groups of four or more, they are called a *gang*. That's only if they are carrying a sharp-edged weapon of some kind, or are *strapped* which we can discuss later I suppose. Notably, when they are all wearing the same primary color this indicates a gang status. If these factors are not mostly or all present, they are simply referred to as *misunderstood*.

SPENCER: A gang of humans? Misunderstood? How do we tell which is which? How can you tell if they have a weapon or not if they are always putting stuff in their pockets?

UTAH: Ok, I'd like to use my active perception surfer skill to analyze where this particular group of humans is along the human *legit-poser spectrum*. I believe you'll find everything you need on page 214 of The Man Manual.

LM: You'll have to come out of hiding in order to do that.

UTAH: Done.

LM: Nice work Spicolli. You detect an 8.9, legit. Way more legit than poser. However, you can tell due to their color coding, although you do not see a weapon present, that they are still possibly misunderstood. As you are taking all of this in, about right now, their leader, the parrot-human, has noticed the last case of beer, and is moving to pick it up. Another of his tribe is reaching in his pocket for something. You're not sure what it is since the pants are sagging so low.

UTAH: Big or small object he's going for?

LM: Could be either. There's a lot of room in there.

UTAH: Pickles. Okay everyone, I'm stepping back now...slowly... Let's just... get back to laying low in this shop. Lots more to find and see anyway. Let's let these groups handle things around that last case of beer. How do we snap McAdams out of his hero dream here Jacoby?

SPENCER: It's too late for that. Listen, save yourselves. Stop the devel-loper, save Matilda's Tiki Bar and keep the file from opening. I'm a goner.

LM: You know what you have to do McAdams.

KAITLYN: No! No, McAdams, don't do it!

SPENCER: I can't. Help. It. I'm compelled by the jacket's increase to my self-importance and irrational human ability to act out what they have seen in *tell visions*. I pick up the goggles of uncertainty and place them securely over my eyes. Then, I remove one of the long spongy hollow pond reeds, and hold it out as a warrior would a magical sword. Finally, I take out one of the spongy shield things and hold it out to protect myself. Then I inch forward, in full view of the gaggling harpy sisters, Bart and the misunderstood and/or gang members. "Yo homeboys," I holler, "These chickens are with me. And so is that last case of beer!"

UTAH: And then there were two…

LM: So, while McAdams is falling into a pit of ruin, what are you doing Utah? Jacoby?

UTAH: Us? I'm staying hidden in the rations aisle, holding onto my lucky turd. I'm going to try to keep my head and my surfboard down low.

KAITLYN: I'm doing the same. I've got Meyers on my human lap, trying to hide behind the shelves of logical items. Oh, I'm also thinking about what I will say at McAdams sentencing. So far, all I have is, "He was born to make a point."

LM: That's not bad actually. Utah and Jacoby, you can no longer see the action. But while McAdams and his jacket of narcissism are consumed by heroism in a beer-related incident, you hear the bell to the logical shop ding once more.

KAITLYN, UTAH: No way!

LM: Yes, way. You hear a voice in a completely new dialect of Eng Lish. "Sheeeeet! San Deego is high steppin' it right now boys!" There's a short pause. Then, another voice but in the same dialect, "Well, well, eve-nin' girls. Eve-nin' fellers." McAdams, you can probably tell that the humans who have just entered are known as...

SPENCER: Rednecks?

LM: Woah! Hold your pixies there. No one said anything about these being red necks. And yes, I do realize that section of Humans and History is getting loads of attention in the chat scrolls these days.

LM: This is a group commonly referred to as *country folk*. Their dialect is very pronounced, thus your passive ability to tell what they are a league away. The four of them are all wearing country folk

garments for male humans: blue jeans, cowboy hats and boots, and patterned crisscross *long sleeve shirts buttoned at the wrist.*

UTAH: Yes, but do they have red necks?

LM: You can't see their necks because of their collars. They are covered.

SPENCER: And I suppose if I try to sniff crotches here that would be inappropriate to at least one of the human subset groups, yes?

LM: Yes. And congratulations you three. About the time McAdams and his jacket here decide to become a hero to the damsels in beer distress, your fate was sealed. It's time to roll initiative!

UTAH: What?! But we haven't even entered debate yet?

LM: You haven't sure. But the swamp doesn't flood just for you now does it?

KAITLYN: Just wow.

LM: Ok friends. Time for a recap. We got Spicolli holding his surfboard, hiding behind the soda potion aisle.

LM: We got Jacoby and Meyers laying low behind him. McAdams is standing his ground directly between the cashier and the sror-tee sisters. The

sisters are all still cackling and grooming their hair simultaneously.

LM: McAdams, you're over here. To your right are the country folk, possible red necks, still standing in the direct path of the sliding glass portal. The chime that announces the door has slid open again is beeping every turn. Besides that beeping sound, it's suddenly very quiet in the shop. The country folk are looking at the sror-tee sisters. The sror-tee sisters are looking at the homeboys. The homeboys are watching the country folk. Bart is watching all of them, from a crouching position behind his counter.

SPENCER: Who's looking at me?

LM: No one.

LM: Bart wipes the bangs out of his eyes. He gulps and says, "Hey y'all. Maybe I can give a discount on some booze in light of it being Sinkody Miyoh and all. What say you all check out the clearance aisle a bit?" He points to the aisle next to where Utah and Jacoby with Meyers are hiding. "Probably everyone'll find what they need!" Utah, you have the next turn. The chime beeps.

KAITLYN: I'm going to delay my action.

UTAH: Me too.

SPENCER: Not me. I'm downing a monster energy potion. Glug. Glug. Glug. How do I feel?

LM: Normal. Might take a while.

SPENCER: Ok. Well, I'm going to then hit my spongy noodle with my spongy shield and make a type of monster roar. Humans don't believe in monsters, but they are afraid of them anyway I read.

LM: You only have two hands.

SPENCER: Oh right. Okay. Just the potion, I guess. Can I do that with two?

LM: Just.

SPENCER: Ok, then I'll wait for my inner monster to arrive and move back a little.

LM: Jacoby? You're up.

KAITLYN: I'm sending Myers around to flank and you see me use my indispensable thumb to grab a can from the shelf. Myers is slinky and stealthy and I am moving next to stand by McAdams. I'm going to attempt to use my last daily to dissuade anyone from getting physical. I'm preparing *jargon* to make an area of logic such that anyone entering it believes the large noodle that McAdams is holding could potentially be threatening, albeit not as a magic sword. Unfortunately, McAdams, you'll still be vulnerable to social or emotional damage inside of my legal orb. I stand tall, lean my chin out and declare, "Look here, peoples! It's Sinkody Miyo! Lots of police people are around. Can you imagine the *jailbond* fees associated with an unintended incarceration? You'd be questing forever just to get out of that pickle."

LM: We'll see how that goes Jacoby, but not a bad turn. Ok, Utah, it's your move.

UTAH: I'm ready! I grab that mysterious little turd, step into the center of the entire fray. Removing it from it's plassed-ticked packaging, I place it directly on the center of the floor with my hand that isn't holding my surfboard. Then, I inhale deeply. I say, "Humans, homeboys, country folk, lend me your two nostrils! Let's all enjoy the bitter and savory aroma of friendship together! My friends and I here only have a couple of moneys but we're on a very noble quest, one in which we do hereby invite you to join! That's right. Join us and rid this quaint seaside town of a foul real estate develloper. Help us save the Tiki Mermaid!"

LM: The bell tolls. "Bro, what?" says a homeboy. And then another homeboy looks as though he's about to answer Spicolli's request, when suddenly his intonation drops.

UTAH: A czar chasm?

LM: That's right! He uses his group ridicule ability! Spicolli, you're immune currently for reasons you are not aware of. Spencer, you're in the direct line of ridicule.

SPENCER: No!

LM: And McAdams, you are now vulnerable both as a hipster and because your social and emotional points are less than 25% of maximum. Stepping forward, the parrot-man points his chin at you. He tilts his head back. He gives three hand chops, then boasts, "Yo homies! Check out little dea-jay-jacket boy over here. You going to go find some beers in the little kiddie pool with your kiddie pool noodle and shit? Huh, little pool boy?"

SPENCER: I'm so down. Had to be a czar chasm, really?

LM: Unfortunately, McAdams, you have just taken 12 points of social damage. As you must have already guessed, you are down. Your sponge noodle goes limp, your spongy shield drops to the linoleum floor. Worse, while the homeboys stand over you, one of them looks over and sees Utah huddling behind his surfboard, holding and sniffing his turd.

UTAH: Spencer's down? For real? He sees my turd?

LM: Yes, for real. Spencer's jacket makes him vulnerable to criticism of a czar's chasm and since you do not have a legitimate background being a hipster class, nor do you have any skill points in rapping, you took double damage. You are currently, lying on the floor in a fawn position, your head in your hands, in a full-blown social ruination and belittling. You've just lost three permanent reputation points as well. Worse, any time in the future, if anyone who observed the social takedown is present, these reputation points will be doubled immediately and applied at any future encounter.

SPENCER: Dang. These homeboys are no joke.

LM: "You ain't seen nothing yet!"

UTAH: What haven't we seen?

LM: No. That's what the leader of the country folk says. He rips off his buttoned shirt, to reveal the exact same type of white undergarment as the homeboys. He then moves to the last case of beer, puts it on his shoulders and spins towards Bart with a folding money in his hands.

KAITLYN: Oh, we can see his neck then! Is it red?

LM: It is! I need everyone who isn't socially ruined and who can see the red necks to roll a redneck-check.

UTAH: What in the forest is a redneck-check?

KAITLYN: I read about this! It depends. Mention certain things like line-dancing, horses, *garth brux*, or numbers like 150, 250 or 350 and you have advantage on certain skill checks against them. But if you fail to mention certain words, you'll have disadvantage and they can become hostile. Also, you got to watch their boots. They're called shit-kickers.

UTAH: What's a *garth brux*? Why would anyone kick shit? I mean, why waste it?

KAITLYN: I'm not sure, but apparently they do. And one part of Humans and History says they can even kick the shit right out of another human.

UTAH: Oh snapping turtle! Can you imagine? Hey, what are the others doing?

LM: The other three rednecks are still standing in the doorway of the shop. The homeboys stand over him, poised to drop more chasm on Spencer McAdams. McAdams, if you take anymore S&E, you'll need to hand me your character sheet. I'm sorry. Bart is still hiding behind the counter. Myer's, the cat, is somewhere, but you aren't sure. The srortee sisters are staring at the case of beer and the shoulder it is resting on, the shoulder of the leader of the red necks. This might actually be an acceptable outcome for you all, except that it's obvious by the looks on the homeboys' faces if the rednecks leave with the beer and the sisters, McAdams is going to pay. You'll also lose logical points because the rednecks have actually created a zone that enhances, rather than dissipates, the sisters' cackling. Therefore, your attempts to free them from their transformation are not going well at all.

LM: The bell chimes again while the other rednecks stand triumphantly, chins up, shoulders back, chests out, hands in their pockets. They are exalted as their leader approaches the counter to pay for the beer.

Except for that, you can hear a leaf blow in the wind. There is unfortunately, nothing stopping the inevitable now. When the redneck leader sets the case on the cashier counter, the beer is his. It's a human cultural rule.

LM: You will then all be charged with a total party bill. McAdams will have to pay for his potion, and possibly for the items he borrowed for the fray. Spicolli, you'll have to pay for what you unwrapped. Sadly team, you will not have enough money to cover all of your expenses and you know what that means- when you're expenses are more than twice your expense portfolio. It's an automatic TPB. This is the end, there's no stopping it.

SPENCER: A TPB already? I can't look.

Chapter 7

Total Party Bill

LM: The leader of the redneck tribe places his beer case on the counter with an impressive *thunk*. Bart smiles.

UTAH: Ritualistic behavior?

LM: Correct! This human ritual signifies that the redneck before you now has rights to this last case of beer. As we have previously discussed, this is a spell of doom for the sror-tee sisters. Ordinarily, the beer may have been shared with them and led to a happy quest outcome for all tribes involved. But sadly, with the homeboys present, the rednecks are simply going to leave the area, and thus leave you all once again on the wrong side of the river. Soon the sror-tee sisters will begin to wail and moan in agony like banshees. This no doubt will affect your social and emotional modifiers significantly. In fact, one of the sisters, she of the twirly finger in her golden hair, gazes down at McAdams, still lying broken and upset on the floor. "I like *thaaaaaawwwwt* you were *liiiiike* gonna help us fricky little pool dude?"

LM: Another of the sisters, she of the river redmud hair, follows her, "*Yaaaaaaah*! Whatha hell?"

LM: And a third, "I. Just. Can't–

UTAH: What about the homeboys?

LM: The homeboys, misunderstood or not, now feel bested by these male rivals. You have in no way endeared yourselves to them at all since McAdams' interruption distracted their ability to use their group tactics against the red necks. Your reputation modifiers have essentially been reduced to zero until you take a long rest. Nor have you done any better with the operator of this shop, Bart. Soon, he will ask you all to pay for the items you have either used, or expended, and you will not have enough money to cover the cost. Your total party bill will thus end the game.

KAITLYN: Total Party Billed.

SPENCER: Again.

LM: Bart reaches out to take the redneck's folding money, which by the way is called *cash*. **You can hear the buzzing of the lick trissity all around you, the monotonous chiming at the door while the triumphant pack of rednecks await their case of beers. Again, this is ritual, people. Very sacred. You can now feel the weight of your inability to change any outcome. It's time, unfortunately my friends, to hand me your character scrolls.**

SPENCER: Niiiiiieeeeehhhhhhhot so fast!

UTAH: Spencer. You don't have to deny it's happening or roleplay through the human cycles of grief in the Library Master's Manual. We've swamp-ruled against that. Game's over.

KAITLYN: Yeah, we'll get them next time Spencer, in another adventure. Here's some dust—

UTAH: Team, I just got a great new quest scroll the other day. Did I tell you? It's called Hang Ten in Hawaii. I can play a surfer again! We all can. Although, I was really looking forward to another human kiss with Selena. I do have to admit. Hey, maybe a certain library master will allow her to play as a non-player human? She is a surf—

KAITLYN: Now we're mixing fantasy and reality. You do know that Selena is real, yes? Here, take my sheet.

UTAH: Mine too.

SPENCER: I said, NOT SO FAST!!!!!!!

LM: What, pray tail are you talking about uni—?

SPENCER: You may still refer to me as McAdams, a level 1 hipster in the real world if you do not much mind!

LM: Okay, if we need to have another talk about reality versus fantasy friends, I am happy to…

SPENCER: Can you please, my good LM sir, tell me what effects the potion of monster energy had on me? I think we skipped over that part, not to put to fine of my point on it.

LM: Well, it's… I am sure it made you….oh my.

SPENCER: Made me, *what now*?

LM: Hang on the tree here…let me just check…the monster energy potion has given you a +3 to mental acuity as well as thirty full minutes of caffeinated absorption. You have gained a type of EHP which I had forgotten about, and it looks as though I'll need to refer to…

UTAH: What in the swamp is EHP?

SPENCER: Extra human perception. There's a chart in the Librarian's Handbook, page 275 if I am not very much mistaken.

KAITLYN: You sir, are not very much mistaken! He's right. I remember that chart last time when I LMed!

UTAH: Right.

KAITLYN: You see, when humans consume vast quantities of a substance called *caffeine*, they become more fully able to access the human skills that each and every class possesses just by virtue of being human. Spencer here has unlocked some of his purest potential as a human by consuming the equivalent of 10 days worth of caffeine in one swallow!

SPENCER: And I intend to use it, people!

LM: McAdams, you can now understand any Eng Lish spoken or written in a 10 foot radius. You also have improved hearing and sight.

SPENCER: I'm scanning both ears and both eyes. Watch me work people. What am I getting?

LM: First, Spicolli's package from the turd of peace he proffered is lying near you. He missed something but in your caffeinated state, you are not missing it! A rune across the front of the package reads, "To activate, place on ground. Then, step on the stink bomb, run and wait for the fun!" There is also an image of a boy holding his nose.

SPENCER: I do it! I step on the turd! Then I hold my nose.

KAITLYN: I'm waiting for the fun!

UTAH: Me too!

LM: Instantly, odoriferous emanations begin to pour out of the small item that Utah thought was just a turd-the one he placed on the ground as a quest offering. All other humans besides you (good job on the nose holding) must now make an immediate save versus *grody* **or instantly puke. McAdams you would have had disadvantage against grody without the nose holding, as all hipsters do. So well done. Utah, surfers urinate in their wetsuits as a way to stay warm. Its also been only 24 hours since you last surfed after a rain event, which means you've developed resistance to sewage. Therefore, you are immune to grody. Jacoby, you'll roll as normal.**

LM: Wow people! Look at you! And I've got even better news. Incredibly the rednecks, homeboys and sror-tee sisters alike have all failed! The sisters are extremely vulnerable to grody, as you all know. The homeboys and rednecks are intoxicated and therefore unable to prevent puking, thus making them vulnerable as well.

UTAH: But none of this matters! The redneck will get the beer. We failed.

LM: Not exactly, Spicolli.

UTAH: What then?

SPENCER: Our rival placed the case on the counter, sure. But the beer isn't his until—

UTAH: Bart takes his money!

LM: Only then will the ritual be complete. And that is the exact moment when Myer's whipping orange and white tail appears over a pack of Bubble Yum and Juicy Fruit. Bart sees the tail, and immediately gushes over the feline's cuteness. He therefore does not see the redneck holding the cash in his hand, nor does he see the man pull his hand back and rush out the glass double doors to puke with his friends in the darkness outside. In an immediate reaction, Bart puts his arms around the case and pulls it back safely across the counter towards his chest. Not to mention that Bart is immune to grody himself due to his experience as an employee of this particular store.

LM: You may find it hard to believe, but the human sense of grody is very different in their world. While you all no doubt would enjoy the sweet savory scent of feces, your characters in human form would not find it pleasant at all and would actually consider it disgusting.

UTAH: Like when someone else pees on my pee bushes?

KAITLYN: Like when my dust gets blown away before landing on the people in whom I wish to give joy?

SPENCER: Like when…hmm.

LM: Yes, similar to those I suppose. So imagine you are reacting in this way. Meanwhile, your adversaries of the debate now flit out the doorway like jungle birds in flight. In succession, one by one, they spill outside and vomit profusely around the shop's entryway. First, the rednecks, leaning over and coughing, collapse through the door. Then, the homeboys, keeping their bandanas over their face like a shield, cascade out like a stream over mossy rocks. Finally, the sror-tee sisters gag and choke on the aroma of the turd, but eventually make their way out, their pony's tails bouncing and swaying behind them. Not only that, but they are no longer giggling even in the slightest, and their perfume, which had nauseating effects of it's own, has cleared from your nostrils, and is replaced by the scent of the so-called "stink-bomb."

UTAH: What is going on???? How is this happening?

SPENCER: That was one incredible logical item.

LM: Bart is staring at you as if you are all...

KAITLYN: Gods?

UTAH: Heroes?

SPENCER: Legends?

LM: Well, yeah, something like that. Bart walks to the door and opens it in an attempt to clear the air, then he moves to the part of the wall alongside where

the counter is and flips up a small lever of some kind. Above you blades begin to spin.

SPENCER: I crouch into a leaping stance!

LM: No. This is not a trap, McAdams. It's something called a *lick-trick fan*. Air blows down from above you, substantially reducing the fragrance along with it. Soon, the aroma around you begins to fade, and you can detect the same odors that you noticed when you entered, stale food mostly. Bart walks up to you, smooths his facial hair, flips his head hear back, and smiles a toothy smile. He rubs a talisman around his neck which is crafted in the shape of a five fingered leaf of some kind. "That was pretty grody dude. But I got to tell you guys, you freaking saved me. Seriously, from like a total nightmare*." He of course is referring to the human habit of having bad dreams during sleep, not the demon horses from the underworld.

LM: "Well none of those three groups are ever a real problem on their own. They're each a different type of person, you know? Just growing and working on themselves like the rest of us humans."

SPENCER: "Yeah, sure I know exactly what you mean, since well, I'm a human myself", I say, and I lean against that stack of boxes arranged like a pyramid.

LM: A few of the boxes fall over, but Bart laughs it off. "Right. But if you hadn't stepped in tonight Pool Warrior, somebody could have gotten hurt, just over a case of beer. All these people come out to have a good time, and on their own they are all usually having a good time. But for some strange reason when they get together, they haven't learned yet how to play nicely with one another. It hurts my heart, dudes. It just seems these days like folks have a hard time understanding that what makes us different as people is like totally okay. I mean that's what Sinkody Miyo is all about. Celebrating our freedom to be our unique selves man. Drink some beer. Eat some *burr ritos*.

UTAH: "I eat burr ritos all the time," I say. "Human burr ritos."

KAITLYN: Its like in our world, you know? Birds of a feather, flock together. Dragons of a color, breathe fire together. I mean, this module is just so deep. I swear, it's got me practically gushing like a freaking human here.

UTAH: Are you getting emotional about humans in the real world, Jacoby?

LM: "Sure," says Bart. "But listen. I'll tell you all what. Since I can tell your heart was in the right place, I won't charge you for that monster energy potion or the stink bomb, k?

SPENCER: "What about these?" I ask, holding up the pool noodle and spongy shield. "A pool warrior needs his pool equipment, no?"

KAITLYN: I hold up the can of snakes! And put the goggles back over my eyes. Wings crossed!

LM: "You guys are crazy, you know that? Listen, you want those items? They'd probably be there for a few more months anyway and we gotta move inventory. Take them. Something tells me that you'll put them to good use, which is more than I can say about 90% of the stuff we sell here."

KAITLYN: He's letting us keep all the loot?!

SPENCER: Snake pit!

LM: Human's say jack pot by the way.

SPENCER: Why does Jack have a pot?

LM: No idea. Just for future reference.

KAITLYN: Well, with this lot of treasure we've got a real chance against the real estate devel-loper. But we'll never get there tomorrow in time to stop the deal from going down. We can't run across an entire country in a day. Nor can we afford a wheeled mount to get to their lair in time before the file of dread opens. It was a great victory tonight, I'm not going to lie. But McAdams takes one more ridiculing and he's pickled. Not to mention the after-effects of his potion are bound to be detrimental, perhaps even game-ending. Myers needs petting. I'm all out of legal jargon and unless Spicolli wants to kiss his way to M&M's lair, we aren't stopping anyone from doing anything in San Deego. What in the nine hells are we going to do with any of this treasure if we can't even get to where the action is?

UTAH: Not to mention we need a long rest.

LM: "Did I hear you guys say y'all need to rest?"

SPENCER: "Yeah, we need to replenish our skills," I respond. "You know, so we can keep bringing the world together." I add casually a, "Right, my man?"

LM: "I totally understand. I wish I had said something earlier. My bad. But say, I got a place out back. Least I can do is offer you guys a place to rest up for the rest of the night. Gotta be out in the morning though, k?"

SPENCER: "You are offering to stand guard while we sleep in your own lair?" I ask.

LM: Bart laughs, "Well, yeah. Sir Bart, at your service! I really appreciate what you lot did to keep things cool."

KAITLYN: I knew he was nobility!

SPENCER: "It's all in a day's human work my new friend. Besides, I am a first level hipster with a focus on brew-making. I can't just stand around while alcohol is abused!"

LM: Bart winks at you, lowers his head and whispers, "Level 1 you said? I think you mean, level 2!"

KAITLYN, UTAH, SPENCER: Snapping turtle!

Level 2

Chapter 8
A Level 5 Conspiracy Theorist

LM: You find yourselves in a truly unique lair, even by human standards. Bart takes you out through the backdoor in the seven-to-eleven, then through a supply room which contains many surplus logical items in boxes made of some strange material. Behind the logical item shop is an empty *pahr king lot*, where a lone yet large yellow mechanical mount sits. It appears to have been there for some time. Bart steps to the front of the giant behemoth. Its two eyes appear open, but they are fixed in a death glare.

KAITLYN: Was it alive before Bart used its corpse for his lair?

LM: No. Human mounts are made of materials like steel and iron metal and plassed tick. But they were never alive.

UTAH: Never alive?

KAITLYN: Mounts made of sword metal? Thats got to take a huge forge! Why not just use horses?

LM: Living things make feces. Humans don't like feces, remember?

UTAH: Wow. I guess not.

LM: Listen, this part of human lore is fascinating, but remember, you can always check out Humans and History. Let's get back to the action.

LM: Bart pulls a lever and a glass partition slides aside, revealing a dark interior with an earthy, leafy smell wafting out at you. Three stairs lead up to the inside of the massive interior. Somehow the bulk of the enormous beast rests atop four wheels made of some strange black substance-in a marvel of human design. Once inside, there's a sort of green mist wafting in the air and this is clearly what is providing the pleasant odor. Above you, the lair's yellow ceiling is slightly arched but is not very tall. The ceiling, like the sides are made of a sun-colored metal and the whole thing shines like the inside of a breast plate due

to the lick trissity from street torches outside. The light reflects around inside giving a dim but warm glow to the space. To either side, blurred by the hanging green mist, there are rows and rows of benches. Above them, on the side walls of the interior are more glass windows. These are much smaller and narrower than the windows you have seen in shops and other buildings. Like the benches, the windows are consistently spaced all the way towards the back of the mount. Yet, most of the windows are covered by murals on paper. On the murals are colorful and brightly painted portraits of various humans, male and female. All of the humans in the paintings appear to be in the middle of consuming small white sticks. The ends of the sticks must have been placed recently in a fire because they are smoking. Green mist hangs around the people inside of their painting worlds.

SPENCER: Is this like a ritual? Why would anyone eat a smoking stick? Just eat a normal one. Sticks are delicious.

LM: Hush. None of you took a background in what humans call smoking or tobacco usage so right now it will remain a mystery of sorts. Besides, I need to read the rest of the description.

LM: Covering the bench seatings and littering the floor of the abode are hundreds and hundreds of empty human food containers. Many are broken and have been flattened into a sort of mesh, like bones in an ancient dragon's lair. The entire lot of them are stacked high in some places. Collectively, they appear to show Bart's diet over time consists mainly of something called a wendy. An image of what may be a wendy appears painted on various worn bags and old smashed paper containers. According to these images, a wendy is a female human with red head hair pulled back into twin braids.

SPENCER: Oh no! I knew it! I crouch again. Team, Bart is a cannibal! He's brought us here to eat us like he eats these wendies. Do I have red hair? I can't remember.

KAITLYN: McAdams. You do have red beard hair but you have no head hair, you keep forgetting. And I'm willing to bet a wing that Bart is not a cannibal. I dumped a few skill points in human cuisine. Wendy is a girl who has a kitchen where humans go to eat quickly. But they do not eat Wendy. Wendy is apparently a very fast cook!

LM: Jacoby is right. And Bart seems to eat almost exclusively this Wendy's fast food. In fact, examining the debris of his eating habits, you notice that there is a particularly worn area down the center aisle between the rows of benches. This seems to be the path that Bart has most often taken when moving through his lair.

SPENCER: Reminds me of that ancient green we had down by the swamp a century back. That's how the warriors found her lair behind the waterfall.

UTAH: Right? I was thinking the same thing.

KAITLYN: Sherserakshen. What a—

LM: Bart tells you that the abode he lives in was once something called a school bus and transported kids from their homes to school. "The wheels on this bus no longer go round and round, my friends," He is giggling to himself as if this is very funny.

UTAH: Are we?

LM: No.

UTAH: Uh, oh. Did he catch what the sisters had? Because if so, we are seriously saddled.

LM: No, he's probably just tired. Humans also love humor, remember. Especially this one. You will too, soon enough...

UTAH: What does that mean?

LM: You'll see.

SPENCER: Are we being trapped? Is this vapor poisonous or something? I'm going to use the last of my logic to detect non-organic chemical compounds. It's an automatic by the way.

LM: Zero. You are all as safe as a sahuagin in a foggy inn here. Trust me.

UTAH: Suuuuuuurreeeee.....

LM: "You guys need a few hits before you hit the sack?" Bart says.

UTAH: "No thanks, human friend," I say back. "We've got plenty of physical points, and we need them all for potential real combat. We need to rest before commencing any training."

SPENCER: I'm looking for sacks to hit.

LM: You don't find any.

LM: "Uh, okay, sure," Bart says. "Whatever dudes. Probably get some residuals anyway." He waves his hand through the air, creating a translucent trail through the vapors temporarily. Bart points to a few areas and tells you where he recommends you make sleeping areas for the night. He reminds you to use the seven-to-eleven's bathroom to "relieve yourself and for other toiletries", and he repeats his command that you must leave by dawn's first light, which he says will have six ayams.

SPENCER: What's an ayam?

LM: It's just a time thing in the real world. After topsun, or what they call "nune" they say there are peeyams.

UTAH: Strange.

LM: Before leaving, Bart's eyes widen. He furls his brows. He leans down a little and speaks in a softer voice. "So are you guys like *really* on a quest?"

UTAH: "Yes," I say emphatically. "We are. We will be ridding this land of a," I lower my own voice to match Bart's, "a greater real state devel-loper."

KAITLYN: "And it's mate."

LM: "Wow," Bart exhales. "You guys are totally legit. I mean, I'm not taking much action these days, granted. I gotta pay the bills and shit, man, you know. But, I do keep up with local action, if you get my drift. We gotta stay on top of *the man*."

UTAH: You do?

LM: "Like yeah, bruh," says Bart. He looks around as if trying to be sure that no other human is in his lair but you all. "I hear all the gossip on the forums, man. You know. Where we go one…" Bart stops, and stares at each of you in turn.

UTAH: What is he waiting for?

SPENCER: There's a shitman?

LM: You need to see Chapter fifteen's sidebar, Differences in Real World Feces. Humans keep their feces to themselves. Even the feces of their familiar. But to answer your first question. He's waiting for you to tell him the second part of the secret code. If

you do, you could unlock some rumors about the area.

UTAH: Oh sweet. We could seriously use these. Everything has happened so fast. We barely know anything about San Deego.

SPENCER: Where we go one…hmmm. I say, "We go on four legs!"

LM: Nope. Try again.

KAITLYN: Snapping turtle! Ok, I say, "Where we go one, we can often be hunted down so its smarter to go as a flock throwing out purple magic dust of camouflage!"

LM: Nope. Now Bart's eyes have narrowed. You seem to be losing some of the trust your previous actions have provided you.

UTAH: This is it. Okay, I say, "Bart, where we go one, we must all of us go together whether we walk on two legs, or four, or use our wings to take us there."

LM: Bart's tightened brow droops, relaxing into a smooth forehead above his hairy lower face. This indicates that you have successfully completed the secret code and have unlocked 1d4+2 rumors, which is…Spicolli's rolling?

UTAH: Four.

LM: Congratulations, you may ask four questions, and receive four rumors! Bart, as you may have guessed, is a conspiracy theorist. A level five conspiracy theorist in fact, which means that his rumors can be quite powerful.

UTAH: Truthful?

LM: No.

UTAH: Complete?

LM: No.

KAITLYN: Got it. I'll go first. I say, "Bart, what can you tell us about the Tiki Mermaid?"

LM: Bart clears his throat. There is a glimmer in his eyes. His tongue darts out, wetting his lips. "The Tiki Mermaid you say? Why, the Tiki Mermaid is one of the proudest establishments in all of San Deego. They've got great craft beer."

SPENCER: Told you.

LM: "Long ago, rumor had it that the Tiki Mermaid had a basement. And in that basement there was a group of runners."

UTAH: Runners?

LM: Runners are simply humans that run as a hobby.

SPENCER: What's a hobby?

LM: Something that humans do when they don't have to do it.

SPENCER: I don't get it.

UTAH: It's a human thing so it won't make much sense.

LM: Bart continues, now in a throaty whisper. "They would run across the city, run back, drink beer until all of the kegs were uncorked. Then, they would plot to do it again!"

SPENCER: "The villains!"

KAITLYN: McAdams, wait. We don't know how true this rumor is. Just because Bart says it is. I mean why would humans run one way, then another, then try and consume all of the beer that a goodly establishment could provide others?

UTAH: Well, it doesn't sound quite humanly possible, that's for sure. But I could see it happening. I mean there were those orcs that one year…"

UTAH: I want to ask about a rumor next please.

LM: Go right ahead. You got three rumors left.

UTAH: "Bart," I say, "We have reason to believe the Tiki Mermaid is the epicenter of something truly dreadful. We believe that there is something called a file, a vile…file…"

KAITLYN: It's a file of dread, Bart.

UTAH: Yes, thank you. A file of dread. And if this file isn't stopped before it opens, then whatever the real estate devel-loper has in mind for the Tiki Mermaid could happen to all of San Deego!

LM: "No way, bro!"

UTAH: "Yes way. You seemed to think earlier that there are divisions in this hamlet, between the tribes I mean. How can we bring these various groups together, under one banner so as to fight against a real estate devel-loper? Surely, there have been other heroes before us who have done so?"

LM: "Bro, that's easy," says Bart, pointing a long finger at one of the murals. A man is eating another of the smoking sticks. He has long hair covering much of his mahogany skin. Runes written under the portrait are easy to read in Eng Lish, "The Kind Will Bring All Mankind Together."

SPENCER: So we are looking for a kind? A kind of what?

UTAH: "Sir Bart, we are planning an assault on the very fortress where the Law Firm of Minick and Minick sits. But we can't do it alone. We need to know how to penetrate their defenses. We need to know how to get inside the file before it opens! And that happens tomorrow when there are nine peeyams."

LM: "Look, I thought I was into some crazy shit, but I see now that you guys are the real deal. I don't really have much in the way to help you guys, and if I borrow any more cash from the drawer I'll be axed for sure, but I do have a couple of old skateboards. Here!" Bart pulls out a couple of wood planks from under a pile of old plassed tick bags. They look like miniature surfboards, but there are wheels on the bottom of them."

KAITLYN: More logical items! This guy is risking getting axed to help us!

LM: "These could help you roll down through the park, then you can wrap along Bahl Boa, and try and get a ride from there to Minick and Minick. If you get up early tomorrow, you could probably make it by nine peeyam."

SPENCER: Bart is seriously like a fairy godfather at this point.

LM: Would you believe that's one of the few things in our world that humans do believe in?

KAITLYN: Ok, everyone be careful here. We have only two rumors left. We can't afford to clean this one up. We know how we can get to M&Ms lair, but boards and minor logical items alone aren't going to be enough to open a dread file. Nor stop these devil lopers once and for all. We need to know how we can defeat them!

SPENCER: Think logical. Think logical.

UTAH: "Bart," I say, "Tell us what you know about Minick and Minick? We have to stop them for good. If what we know is true, then what is happening at the Tiki Mermaid is even worse than what you imagined. Surely, you have heard something about them that can aid us on our quest."

LM: Bart gives you your third rumor, only one left. "Well, there was a thread that I was checking out, just last week actually. One of my…colleagues…said he was a city planner for a grip of years. He was claiming that the land around the Tiki Mermaid was actually quite special. Some creek system feeds into the sewer right underneath it. Because the Tiki Mermaid hasn't fully used up all of that land, the earth around the building acts like a filter, keeping the toxins from entering the San Deego Bay. The ground there literally siphons off all the bad stuff right into the sewer where it gets treated properly. The Tiki Mermaid is basically a natural water filter. There's no telling how accurate the guy is though, or if he really is who he says he is. So, I fully believe him myself. Say, you guys sure you don't want to take a few hits?"

KAITLYN: Toxins? So that's the plan. The devel-lopers plan to poison the San Deego bay. Think of all the humans and nonhumans too that will be affected!

UTAH: And once the bay is poisoned, the devel-lopers can move in, and spread their evil spawn throughout the city!

KAITLYN: Tackses.

UTAH: Stripping Malls.

SPENCER: Gardens of Olives. It will be a hellscape!

LM: "Man," says Bart, "You guys really look stressed. You sure you don't want to take a few hits before hitting the sack yourself?"

KAITLYN: Okay, everyone. We have one rumor left. This one is critical. Every human think about how we need to…

SPENCER: I have to know what sack Bart is referring to! There must be something special in it.

LM: Do you wish to ask him?

SPENCER: Yes.

LM: That is your fourth rumor. The sack he is referring to is any area where one lays down, which could be a bed, a sack of potatoes, or even just the floor.

UTAH, KAITLYN: Snapping turtle! You tricked him!

LM: I'm a library master. It's my job to trick you. Bart smooths back his hair and gives you all a wave of his hand, a gesture of goodbye. "It's been real dudes. But I gotta get back to the store. I'm doing an all-nighter, but I'll check in on you all so you can all get some sleep back here without being disturbed.

Best of luck on your quest tomorrow." And he steps out, closes the glass partition, and walks back into the shop. The inside of the lair grows darker now without the light from the open doorway.

KAITLYN: We were so close.

LM: My friends, don't pull your own tails. You didn't do half bad. Most human teams do not get more than one or two rumors out of Bart, and you got three. Besides, it is time to level up! Utah, let's check in with you first.

UTAH: Well, I get a few bonuses. For one, I don't need normal rations. I can survive on beer and burr ritos alone for up to a full season if necessary. I also get a +1 to all physical skills and a +2 now when I use *bro* in place of a name with any layman. There's also a host of physical things I can do that involve balance and wait until you see me use this surfboard. Plus, I speak *Dude*.

KAITLYN: What's Dude?

UTAH: It's a language that's popular in San Deego. You'll see. Very universal.

LM: You have also gained proficiency with boards of *skay ting*. **How's that for timing? Okay Jacoby. I'm guessing that you're sticking with a legal subclass of logic-user, 2nd level?**

KAITLYN: You are correct in that assessment my good sir. And if you're wondering why I sound so formal, allow me to explain Your Honors! At level two, I can take both a daily of *injury liability persuasion* and I can even create a *zone of jargon*.

UTAH: What does a zone of jargon do?

KAITLYN: It's a nice diversion basically. I don't want to give too much away until I get to use it! But that's nothing compared to what I'll be able to do if I make it to third level!

UTAH: Oh yeah. That's when you get *cone of code switching*, right?

SPENCER: Yep. It's a total game changer when Jacoby fires that baby off.

LM: Anything else?

KAITLYN: Not much. Meyers is able to hide anything flat by lying on it with his body for a couple of rounds. But that's about it.

LM: Sounds good. Well, finally the hipster. Are we still going with another level of craft brewer, McAdams?

SPENCER: Nope. Surprise. I've been taking notes. Clearly being knowledgeable in beer is extraordinarily helpful in human society but I've been doing some reading in the chat scrolls.

UTAH: Here we go…

SPENCER: There's a new subclass of hipster. It looks pretty interesting.

LM: And I suppose you assumed it would be LM approved?

SPENCER: Well, I had hoped you might approve of a level in *rhetorical hipster*.

UTAH: What's rhetoric? Is it like logic?

KAITLYN: Oh, it's so exciting. It's completely new. Logic is of course a human's primary weapon, and defense. Logic is what humans use to get the job done, as they like to say. But rhetoric is what they use to make their job look done, whether it is or not.

UTAH: Humans can do that?

KAITLYN: Oh yeah. And hipsters aren't the only ones. Many think that rhetoric could be a subclass for just about any type of human.

UTAH: Wow. So, what can you do with this new rhetoric of yours? Provided our wonderful LM agrees to this subclass of course…

SPENCER: Well, it's a bit tough to describe. Might have to wait until you see it in action.

LM: Or until I approve it. Which if it's in action, will be too late, won't it?

KAITLYN: Oh, you know you're gonna. Seriously.

LM: I do? Look, *people*. Here's what I do know. You've all got, as Bart would say, a grip of new skills and abilities, not to mention logical items that would make any human layman envious. But none of it matters unless you take a long rest. So, sleep. I give you my LM guarantee that Bart has your back and will not cannibalize you the way he did Wendy.

SPENCER: I knew it!

Chapter 9

The Great Tomithino

KAITLYN: So, it's like flying? Like flitting from tree to tree?

LM: Not exactly.

SPENCER: Like galloping through a moist meadow after a rain has made the earth springy under hoof?

LM: Sorta.

UTAH: Like slipping down a rain-soaked grassy knoll, twirling nose over tail and falling into a pond?

LM: I suppose you could think of it that way.

UTAH: And the things under us are turning?

LM: Yes, they're called *wheels* and they go around and around, which causes your speed to increase the more they turn.

UTAH: Do not get any of that, but I am going as fast as I can then.

KAITLYN: Me too.

SPENCER: So, am I. Wait, I am on Spicolli's back right? Can you imagine, me on a back?

LM: Correct, and Meyer's is tucked snuggly into a sack over Jacoby's shoulder. His purring is soft so you can tell that he's content. Your other gear is all secured in similar sacks on your person. Utah and Jacoby are in control of the two skay-ting boards. You use your back foot to steer and your front foot to push.

SPENCER: Your back *foot*. Your front *foot*. So weird.

UTAH: And we're going very, very fast.

LM: That's all correct. But let's recap first. Arising before the sun, you…

UTAH: Did you say Sun*uh*?

LM: Yes. There is only one Sun in Real World.

KAITLYN: You see, that's just bad game design. As soon as anyone hears that they know you can't just have one sun. I mean how would you know when to sleep, *again*?

LM: For the last time, I did not design the real world. I just describe it. Someone needs to refer to their Human Handbook. Page 34 I should think. And now…Arising before the sun*uh*, you bid Bart farewell. For some reason, he doesn't seem to have a problem when you sniff his butt.

SPENCER: I really like that human. I hope we see him again.

LM: You are *skay-ting* down the foothills of San Diego's golden hills neighborhood. From Utah's background you gathered that you needed to use foot power to make the logical item go forward, unless it was going downhill. And you also chose to ride on the part of the human roads known as *sidewalks*, slick stone surfaces that go on and on until there is a crack and then you all fall over in a heap. But you get up quickly enough and continue on your journey. Which is good, since massive four wheeled mounts roll by you at high velocity. Each is like a much larger version of the boards you now ride, but with a compartment inside where humans sit and stare out of the windows.

LM: To your left is San Deego Bay, bright, expansive. You see hills of orange flame at its shores, and beyond the expansive crystal blue sea as far along the horizon in both directions as can be seen. The hills are speckled with human dwellings, various versions

but with the same general shape of those you now pass.

LM: Ok. So human dwellings are whizzing by like elvish arrows, and every so often you fall over or you have to swerve a little to avoid a human child, or a human walking alongside a wolf, which humans have turned into much stupider and weaker versions called dogs.

KAITLYN: Some humans can be wicked at times, you–

LM: Just then! Overhead, a massive form, wings outstretched, glides over you. It blocks the sun, roars in hunger, and plunges you into shadow!

KAITLYN, UTAH, SPENCER: Dragon!!!!!

LM: The beast is right on top of you. There's no where you can run, or hide, or jump. You are–

KAITLYN: Doomed?

UTAH: Pickled?

SPENCER: Pond scummed?

LM: The victim of not reading your handbook again! This is a plane of celestial air! It's a mount that humans use to travel vast distances.

SPENCER: Does it eat us though?

LM: No. You are not the prey it wants. Like the mounts whizzing by you on tires, it only drinks.

KAITLYN: Blood?

LM: No. No one here took any skill points in human transportation, so it will remain another mystery.

UTAH: But we're safe, yes?

LM: Yes, you are safe. In fact, while the aerial monstrosity flies over you, the wheels on your board roll less and less. You've come to the bottom of golden hill! You have made terrific progress, and you have reached the first marker on your journey to the law firm of M&M. Refer now to your San Deego map and find the location, "Bahl Boa Park."

LM: Before you there are large white stoned temples on well-kept grounds of green grasses, flowering bushes and majestic trees. This is clearly a sacred complex of some kind. There are many humans wandering around as though they are in deep thought. Most of them are eating or drinking from various containers. More of the fast food perhaps. But these are made by someone named Mack Donald, and another, the son of Carl.

UTAH: Gods of food?

KAITLYN: Woah. It's like those we found in Bart's lair. Was Wendy someone who had worshippers? Followers?

LM: That would be accurate, yes.

UTAH: Cultists of Carl? Acolytes of Arby's? Zealots of the golden arches?

LM: Perhaps.

UTAH: Hmmmm….so mysterious. Does anyone among these worshippers stand out from the pack?

LM: As a matter of fact, yes. Not far from your position now, over a small grassy knoll, there is a halfling wizard on some type of raised platform in front of a flowering rose garden. He is being swallowed by a magnificently colored robe and wizard's hat. On his shoulder sits a green dragon hatchling. The wizard has attracted a large crowd of excited onlookers while he casts spells. The crowd gasps sporadically.

KAITLYN: What in the name of Mordenkainen?

UTAH: Wait. This is a setup, right? I walk towards the performance and use my surfer social ability to blend in with the crowd.

KAITLYN, SPENCER: Me too.

LM: You approach the scene and attempt to ratnose your way from the back of the crowd to the front. The humans around you gasp collectively two more times. Arriving in the front nearest to the platform, you can see that the halfling has hung a sign under an

ingeniously designed, temporary stage. The runes say in Eng Lish, "The Great Tomithino! Tips or you'll be turned into a pixie!"

KAITLYN: Why I never! You did that on purpose, right?

UTAH: The Great Tomithino? What kind of wizard name is that?

LM: Quiet. The wizard is about to perform more magic. He clears his throat and pushes his sleeves back. The crowd grows quiet with anticipation. "I will now perform an incredibly strong piece of magic! Therefore, so that my head does not explode, I beg you all to stay absolutely silent. Remember, The Great Tomithino risks all, *all* for your viewing pleasure!" He bows serenely, but just deep enough so that the little green hatchling doesn't fall off his shoulder. In one swift motion, The Great Tomithino removes his hat and extends it to the crowd upside down. A few people place coins and bills into it.

KAITLYN: Magic for money?

LM: The wizard shakes his hat a bit, and there's a rattle of coins. He grins slyly. Then he puts the hat back on his head without anything falling out. This in and of itself seems to please the crowd. He expounds, "The Great Tomithino will now delve into the powers of the primordial! From the ancient wisdom of bygone lore, I will use *real* magic to make one lucky volunteer completely disappear! Do I have any volunteers from the audience? Anyone? Anyone? Ah, you ma'am! Please, step forward. Step forward!" Kaitlyn Jacoby, he is pointing at you!

KAITLYN: At me?

LM: What do you do?

KAITLYN: What do I do? Ha. I should ignore him so he can turn me into a pixie!

UTAH: Good one.

KAITLYN: Fine. I'll go up there. But if I disappear because of his *real* magic in the *real* world, then I think I should get to make myself reappear like in ours.

LM: Deal. You step onto the stage Jacoby, and you can now tell that this halfling is nothing more than a very short middle-aged human who for once doesn't smell so bad. He's got sort of a whiff of delightful body odor, mixed with fermentation of food, drink, and urine upon his garments. He leans into you, and whispers into your ear so that only you can hear, "There's a compartment under us. You look a bit down on your luck. When I cause the diversion, crawl into it and out behind the rose bushes. Come back in an hour and I'll give you twenty bucks."

KAITLYN: Twenty bucks! That could pay for a private mount to the law firm.

SPENCER: Tomithino is our fairy god-halfling!

LM: "NOW!" Yells The Great Tomithino to his audience. The small crowd has now swelled in size to nearly a hundred humans. "BEHOLD as this young lady bravely ventures into the void. Fear not my friends, for although you shall not see her again this day, I shall conjure her back to our world once more, when my powers have been rejuvenated. And when she does return to us, she will have seen the *other* side. The world of the magical! The world from which I have been many times myself!"

LM: There is a flash and thick smoke billows from his sleeves. It quickly fills the stage area and obscures you, Kaitlyn, from any view in the audience. Now you hear a small click, and then you are pushed down below the stage. It is cramped and dark, yet otherwise you are safe. Above you, the Great Tomithino carries on. "BEHOLD! She has gone on to the other side."

LM: There is a smattering of applause and you can hear the clink and chink of coins falling on coins. The Great Tomithino carries on while you follow a small opening in the back of the stage. Crawling through it, you exit out beyond the rose garden on the other side.

UTAH: But we don't know she's there right? I mean all we see is the Great Tomithino or whoever finish up his trick of magic–

LM: Peace. During the show, Meyers jumped from her arms. You see his tail slinking behind a rosebush thick with lush red roses. Following the cat, you find Kaitlyn behind the rosebush.

UTAH: Awesome. If we just wait until Tomithino pays us, we'll be set! We can pay for a mount to take us to the law firm and face the devel-lopers before the file opens!

LM: Right. This is a good stopping point if anyone needs to shake some dew from their lilypad or knock a bit of bark off their tree. We've been going nonstop for almost two of the suns' sets.

KAITLYN: Okay, perfect. I've got to check-in on some eggs anyway.

*   *   *

UTAH: So, what did I miss?

KAITLYN: Thank the pond, Utah's back!! Where have you been?

UTAH: I was just…what is happening? Why is the LM smiling?

LM: Welcome back Utah Spicolli. I'll review a little of your predicament for my own pleasure.

UTAH: Lovely.

LM: As you know Kaitlyn Jacoby did not disappear because of actual magic. She agreed to become an accomplice in a pretend magic show and snuck under the stage during Tomithino's diversion. Crawling out beyond the rose bushes, she attracted Meyer's attention. You followed Meyers and awaited your payment. However, one of Tomithino's acolytes, a bespectacled human child named Nora, followed the cat and you, and discovered Kaitlyn Jacoby's trickery. Humans do not like being made a fool. Especially when their money is involved. Human debate commenced, and at some point, The Great Tomithino somehow convinced his followers that Kaitlyn Jacoby was up to no good.

KAITLYN: The great *rogue*, Tomithino!

LM: The party was thus pursued over the grounds of this vast temple complex.

UTAH: So where are we now?

KAITLYN: We managed to escape the crowd by hiding behind an area of *eye scream*.

UTAH: Eye scream?

KAITLYN: Yeah. but we learned that the screaming comes later. Humans seem to enjoy consuming this creamy filling of frozen cow's milk in a crispy conch that is very cold and gives you headaches. This in turns brings on the screaming after your head is ripped into two frozen pieces. McAdams failed his save versus snackage and spent the last of our coin on a large eye scream.

SPENCER: I'm sorry Utah. I couldn't help—

KAITLYN: Don't blame yourself McAdams. I'd scream, you'd scream. We'd all scream, for eye scream.

LM: After that, the party attempted to blend in with the cultists and followed a stream of humans into one of the larger human temples seeking divine grace. But that's not what *you're* going to find here.

UTAH: Uh oh.

LM: You have now entered The Museum of Natural History.

UTAH: Natural?

LM: You stand in the center of a grand hall, worthy of a dwarven king. All around you, erect and serene are the skeletons of massive and fantastical dragons which the humans have reconstructed in various attack postures using cleverly designed systems. The bones are arranged and held in place by metal fasteners and wires hanging from a vaulted ceiling above. Many small humans gather around the skeletons gawking and gesturing towards the remains of these magnificent and ancient creatures.

UTAH: So, let me get this straight–

LM: Go on.

UTAH: Dragons once ruled the real world too?

LM: Correct. Sort of.

KAITLYN: All types. Sea. Land. Air?

LM: Yes.

UTAH: But then humans came along. And the dragons did not eat them all?

LM: There were too many humans. Not enough dragons.

KAITLYN: So, the humans lived, but the dragons died out?

LM: That's what the adventure background says.

UTAH: And now the humans use dragon skeletons to what, scare little humans into obedience?

LM: Look, there is actually a group of small humans with a parental figure near a dragon skeleton at the present moment if you'd like to investigate.

UTAH: I would. Indeed.

LM: The first thing you notice is that the wyrm they are near had been a magnificent specimen. But then, looking up through the bony ribs, you can see that the skeleton is incomplete. The dragon stands on two

legs, a gaping jaw reaching out on a long neck as if it could still catch prey. Its tail is whipping behind it, but there are no wings attached to the shoulders where a dragon's wings should be. Perhaps, like many of the other dragon skeletons in the hall, they were no longer intact when the body was discovered. You find the wingless dragons fascinating, but you hear the children speaking so you listen in. A small human child is tugging on the sleeve of his older human father.

LM: "Daddy!" He cries in pure joy. "Where'd the *tee rex* go?"

KAITLYN: The name of this beast while it lived, so sayeth the runes on this plaque.

LM: The father answers, "Son, the tee rex was wiped out by the ass droid."

LM: "Daddy, what's a…ass droid?"

LM: "Hmmm. Imagine a gigantic, burning, fiery, hurling chunk of…"

LM: "Excuse me," says a feminine voice from behind you. The father's story drifts from your consciousness. You spin around to see a female human wearing a blue uniform with a badge on her chest.

SPENCER: Excellent. I'd like to ask her about the—

LM: Sorry McAdams. This female guardian does not look happy in the slightest. She is immune to the challenge.

KAITLYN: The mob watching Tomithino's performance must have summoned her. We're in for it now.

LM: "You can't bring--well you can't bring *any* of those things in here." She points to Spicolli's surfboard, to your skay-ting boards, to Spencer McAdams boogie shield and sponge sword, and to Meyers who is poking his head out of Kaityln's backpack. There's the slightest hint of amusement on her face now. "Yeah, not *any* of that is okay here folks. You'll need to go. Like, now." She points her finger to a large set of doors at the other end of the hall.

KAITLYN: Thank Greyhawk. Let's obey and get out of this accursed temple complex before we lose any more time or money.

SPENCER: But I just need to know about the ass droid. I mean anything that could kill dragons, right? It has to be something that the devel-lopers would fear.

KAITLYN: Well, according to the Humans and History glossary, humans nearly always refer to an ass as both their buttocks and anus combined. And it says here that a droid is a metal version of a human which is built to perform a particular function, often mimicking human behavior. I can't imagine that a mechanical human ass eliminated all the dragons!

SPENCER: It's not much to go on. There has to be more to what the ass did.

LM: And unfortunately, the father and son have moved off so this particular part of human lore will remain a mystery to you. "Time to go," says the guard, now impatient with her hand hovering over something on her utility belt. Remember also that any human law enforcement has the power to conjure a nearly unlimited amount of reinforcements and very quickly.

SPENCER: "We'll go. I promise," I say. "Just can you tell us one thing?"

LM: She doesn't look like she is in the least bit interested in obliging you McAdams, but she is for some unknown reason still looking at you. This is a human sign she may answer one question you have if you agree to leave exactly as she requests.

SPENCER: Okay, we begin to walk towards the hall exit as she requests. But before I leave, I ask, "Could you please tell me how your hot ass was able to wipe out–"

Chapter 10

I Wish a Carron Would

SPENCER: What happened?

KAITLYN: You were critted, physically critted, and knocked completely unconscious. We dragged you out of the dragon shrine hall to the shade of this magnificent tree.

UTAH: You're lucky to be alive. Again.

KAITLYN: I wonder if the magical part of Kaitlyn misses being in a tree?

LM: We discussed not crossing fantastical-reality barriers at the log, remember? Realize after the game please. So just to recap, *again*, you are all lucky to

still be alive, free, and not psychologically damaged beyond all recognition. You have spent the last of your money on eye scream but gained no noticeable effects. McAdams is still cursed with narcissism and is low in almost all areas of human endeavor: social, emotional, physical and of course financial. Meyers is getting hungry, and Kaitlyn and Utah have two skayte boards and one surfboard between them. You've got a ways to go to get to the law firm but now the sun is at the midpoint of its arc in the sky. You're going to have to find a way to get to the next stop on Bart's map, and quickly.

KAITLYN: But how do we get out of these temple grounds?

UTAH: I'll try an ocean-locator investigation check to get us back on our boards, and down a hill so we can let our wheels spin again. I cup my hand to my puny human ear and listen.

LM: Well, you have human ears so you aren't hearing a lot, just so we are clear. But you can tell, even at a distance, that although the area seems peaceful, there is a commotion near a magnificent fountain which is located in the middle of a plaza at the center of multiple temples. This area is also marked on your map so there may be a clue there about which way to go.

UTAH: Said every LM setting a trap, ever.

SPENCER: What's going on? How can we help?

LM: There appear to be some small humans in the pool at the center of the fountain. Other larger humans standing around the fountain are yelling at them in some form of broken Eng Lish. Yet more small humans are moving around the larger ones in a wide circle. The last group appear to be using wheels due to their speed. In wide arcs they circle the pool. These latter humans are clearly chanting for the young males in the water to continue their water activities, while the elder and larger humans clearly want it to cease.

KAITLYN: This sounds like deleek wents! They'll know how to get out of the grounds and down the rest of the way towards Lah Hoya! How do we approach them though? What should we do?

LM: I don't know. What should you do?

KAITLYN: This is exactly what he says when he wants us to stop and interfere, when we should probably keep going. However, there's probably more treasure here. I smell treasure here.

UTAH: You smell treasure at every encounter.

KAITLYN: That's because there almost always is!

UTAH: Okay. I'll take your bait. I hop on my *skayte* board, swerve over to the fountain, use my kick-flip daily to jump off, help McAdams land on his two human feet, all while simultaneously keeping the board in control. Then I take in the scene a little more. What's going on exactly in this sacred fountain?

LM: Impressive moves. First, the fountain and pool are large, about the size of a small beaver pond. In the middle, a geyser of water shoots up to the height of a middle-aged willow tree. Dancing around the geyser, in water that is up to their knees, are three young male humans, two with long hair that reaches almost to their buttocks. The last, who seems to be the leader, has a spiky ridge running along the mid-lateral line of his head down to his spine. Screaming into the fountain, at the boys, are three much older human females. They are pointing shaking fingers at the boys in the water, as though cursing them with magic spells. Their fangs are out, mouths agape, assaulting their prey with wicked jeers.

UTAH: A witches coven!

KAITLYN: Or maybe reality hags?

SPENCER: Urban banshees?

KAITLYN: No friends. I know what these are. And we're in for it now. These are carron crawlers!

SPENCER: What's a carron crawler?

LM: As if in answer to your question, the three females creep closer to your position using their immediate reactions to involve themselves in affairs that have nothing to do with them. It's a lair action.

You can now discern that each has heavily coated pale faces with a type of war-paint that human females call *make up*. There is red paste smeared over their taught lips and a blood red cloud of mud rubbed into their cheeks. Their eye lashes have grown considerably longer, perhaps due to some transformation they have endured. The most notable aspect to them is their hair style. Each has bushy, curly hair, as though a pair of swamp stirges decided to build a nest on their heads. One pushes a small stroller in which a miniature short-haired wolf-creature with no discernible eyes due to the hair covering its face is sitting upright and snarling.

UTAH: I thought strollers were for small humans.

LM: They are.

KAITLYN: Weird.

LM: "Hush, Ginger!" Says the woman behind the stroller. She holds her flabby chin high and pounds her flabby fists against her thighs like an albino jungle gorilla. "Baby, these boys clearly don't know that Mama is president of the Golden Hills Pee Tee Aay. Not today. Uh uh. Not on my watch you, deleek wents."

LM: "Becky, would you look at this. Gee Yosephat. Now three more of the little devils just showed up," says a second, her nostrils flaring in and out. Her head hair is cut very short, and fits like a warrior's helm, covering her entire head, except the bare skin of her face in front.

LM: The third and largest, her small blue eyes turning red around the pupils, bellows at you in a type of battle cry. She blinks rapidly and runs her painted fingernails through her head hair in some sign of passive human aggression. "My father sits on the board of directors for Bahl Boa Park. And I am going to tell you all," she swirls her other pink taloned finger in the air, "one last time. Either walk those boards on outta here, or we're going to call for *see curity*."

LM: "And the manager," says the second woman gnashing her teeth. There are sweat beads now along her thin nose. "The see curity manager!"

LM: The little wolf-creature yaps and the larger lady behind the stroller puffs out her well-endowed bosom, "You do not mess with the founding members of the Mission Hills Rose and Tea Society."

LM: This is clearly a magnificently performed human threat and display of rhetorical prowess! Nevertheless, there's a collective snort and snicker from the crowd of young people, both in the water, and around the fountain. In one motion, like a pack, the deleek wents flip up their boards and tuck them under one of their two arms. Those in the water, all hop out, and finding their boards, join the others in solidarity. It looks as if the young humans are going to stand their ground.

UTAH: Wow. Would you look at them move together as one.

LM: "Calm your tits Carron!" Says a deleek went near you.

LM: "Yeah, simmer down you stankass grannies," chimes another while a relaxed smile crosses his face. This too, is a form of passive human aggression.

SPENCER: Does it do damage?

LM: Not exactly. But it lowers a victim's immunity to other attacks. Like czar chasms, rhetoric, and mockery.

SPENCER: Wow.

LM: Yeah. The deleek went skay-ters continue their verbal assault. There's a charge in the air, as if lightning had just struck a nearby tree. "*Skay Ting* is not a criminal. We've got a right to be here too. So do they!" He points at the lot of you all, having just arrived in the center of the fray. It is clear now that the carron crawlers have been offended. And you are part of the offense offending them.

UTAH: What's offended?

KAITLYN: Uh oh. Offended is a type of rhetorical attack humans think can hurt them, although it can't. It's sort of like an illusion in our world. But carron crawlers do not like to be offended. They are highly vulnerable, and will take emotional damage, illusion or not. But that damage comes with a side-effect.

SPENCER: I wish a carron would—

LM: "Help!" They all begin to yell in unison.

LM: "Help, we're being harassed!" Yells the first.

LM: "I don't feel safe!" Yells the second. She steps just a little too close to your pool noodle McAdams, and hits her head on the instrument. "Ouch! Assault! I've been assaulted!"

SPENCER: No, she hasn't.

LM: "Get away from me!" Yells the third now with tears streaking her war paint. The great rivulets of black and red are cascading down her chubby cheeks. "Get away from me, all of you." You can now feel the little human hairs on the backs of your necks stand up. Around you, hundreds of the food-worshipping cultists pause between bites and turn in your direction like bees to a blossom. Then they began to shamble towards you, eyes wide, mouths chewing food rapidly so they can use verbal attacks if need be. The carron crawlers have used their combined social connection as an immediate reaction lair action to the offending. Dozens of summoned do-gooder humans are making their way towards the center of the fountain plaza now to investigate what is going on. The carron crawlers each point a sharp finger directly at you!

LM: "Hey," yells a male human. "That's the girl who pretended to disappear with that phony magician and took my money!"

KAITLYN: Uh oh.

LM: "They've got skayte boards! All of them! And these older ones too. The signs are right there! Right there!"

LM: "This is why we can't have nice things!" Says the second.

LM: "They *threatened* us. Call see curity! Call a manager!" Shouts the third. You're now surrounded by their minions. Many of these humans are large males. Here in certain parts of the real world, large males will protect female humans if they believe the offenses to them are legitimate, especially when they have the abilities of a carron. Running may be hazardous to your physical health so do consider your actions carefully.

KAITLYN: Well, that's super bad! I mean we can't allow them to take our boards. That would be a disaster, especially now that we have no money left. I could try my rhetoric?

UTAH: No. You must not! We need to save that for the devel-lopers.

SPENCER: What about your legalese Jacoby?

KAITLYN: Are you kidding? Even at level two, I'm no match for the jargon power of three fully formed carron crawlers!

UTAH: But we've got to, we've got to at least try!

LM: Several of the deleek went skay-ters around you have tried to escape through the reaching clutches of the food cultists. A few made it, rolling away on their boards with expert foot power.

UTAH: Can I see which way they are headed? Can we follow?

LM: You can tell which way they go, but you won't be able to sneak past these humans like the others did. Skay-ter stats are insane for quick escapes.

LM: Several however don't make it and are caught by male humans now looking to their carron overlords. The lot of you, about a half dozen skay-ters, and your party of would-be San Deegan heroes, are utterly surrounded. The entire ensemble of cultists looks to the carrons-awaiting their next command. These creatures are squealing with delight. Inside the little baby carriage, the tiny wolf creature yips and yaps.

LM: In clear triumph, the first carron thrusts out her bosom and commands maniacally, "This is a park for families! This is a park for law-abiding citizens! We have rules for a reason here. We have rules to keep people–"

LM: "DUDE!" Yells one of the skay-ters, interrupting the carron.

SPENCER: What's a *dude*?

LM: "DUDE!!!!" The skay-ter is now pointing at a sign near the fountain, and another is pointing to you, Spicolli. It's the same sign that the carron was pointing towards while commanding her legions. Its literally covered in small runes.

KAITLYN: What's this little male doing? Is he hoping to cause a diversion? Trying to counter with legalese? Obviously, it's not even a skillset that–

UTAH: There's no way we can decipher all that anyway. Kaitlyn, can you tell if this boy is some kind of legal expert in disguise?

KAITLYN: You mean a dobble gangster? Highly unlikely. Most likely he understands that in human culture adults will not respond well to an argument made by a child. He sees us, in our young adult bodies and he is trying to get our help. But, I don't even speak Dude so it wouldn't help anyway. I mean, dude is a very rare language and is most often spoken by skay-ters but sometimes by–

LM: Surfers?

UTAH: Oh snapping twigs! It's an automatic part of the surfer sub class. I speak Dude fluently at level 2!

KAITLYN: Which is probably why he is pointing at you Spicolli standing there holding a surfboard.

UTAH: Well, what is he saying to me?

LM: Since you are fluent, here's your direct translation: Good day partners in righteousness. I beg assistance from you in order to debate these foul carron crawlers at a level which they will understand. Will you grant me your assistance?

SPENCER: All that?

LM: Yep. Dude is a very concise linguistic form. Spicolli, your reply?

UTAH: Like dude, right on, but *dude*?

LM: The skay-ter understands.

KAITLYN: Understands what exactly?

UTAH: I replied with: Hello fellow thrillseeker, I'd be glad to help you in any way I can. Please specify what you need and I will give it my full attention.

LM: Correct translation Utah, well done. Someone has been studying his Dude. The lead Skay-ter, he of the spiny hair, then points his finger again at the sign, "Dude!"

LM: Translates to, "Thank you comrade. As you can clearly see from this sign, the carron crawlers are using legalese to keep my fellows and I from enjoying

ourselves here. We apologize for getting you involved as we were just having a bit of fun. Nevertheless, us being younger, we cannot effectively debate with such a foul beast on level terms. However, I noticed that there are runes which pertain to the carron crawlers themselves. Would you be so kind as to point this out to them, being the adult that you are?"

UTAH: My reply: Like dude. No worries bro.

LM: You're giving assistance?

UTAH: Kaitlyn Jacoby, would you be so kind as to find and decipher verbally the runes on the plaque that pertain to carriages for human children.

KAITLYN: Huh? Uh, yeah, sure. Do I–?

LM: You're level two. It's an automatic.

KAITLYN: Oh wow. Well, I, oh wow. Get ready everyone, this is going to be good. I use *legalese* and *jargon expert* to expel a range of social debate up to a 40 foot radius. Back straight, human body tall to make myself look more intimidating to the attackers, I expel my jargon!

KAITLYN: "Hear me Cultists of the Carl! And of his junior! Acolytes of the sippy beverage and of the elongated fried potato wedge. Lickers of the eye scream, heed me! You have been falsely summoned to this fountain to do the bidding of these foul creatures, those three of the helmeted hairstyle, of the smeared war paint who would savagely assault smaller human children in the name of their own see curity and satisfaction. But behold! Upon this sacred plaque it has been foretold that any carron who would desanctify these sacred temple grounds by pushing around a carriage in which not a child rests, but a miniature wolf-beast yips and yaps, must they themselves be taken henceforth from this place. Upon this sacred written pact, you are foresworn."

KAITLYN: I then flit over to the carriage, and peel back the cover for even more dramatic effect!

LM: Lots to unpack here, but bravo! First, you are not flitting. You are walking, just to clarify. Second, the miniature wolf-creature is revealed, which if you have seen the latest article in People, Pets and Parties Magazine, you will know is called a "cheewha--labra-doodle-collie puppy." This is a difficult animal to breed and care for, so it is most likely used as a deliberate sign of the wealth of this carron. But more to the point, your attack has had an immediate effect! Every single one of the acolytes has returned to slurping, shuffling, and shambling around the grounds again, as if you were never there.

KAITLYN: But what about the three crawlers?

LM: Oh, you'll love this part. Your skay-ter comrade is so impressed with your attack, Jacoby, that he removes a small black rectangular device from his garment pocket and holds it out to the nearest carron. With frightening shrieks and a unified threat

to continue this battle in someplace called a "courtalaw" all three of the carrons use their park camouflage and slink back away and out of sight.

SPENCER: Wow. Seriously, if I had hands, I would be clapping like a human right now.

UTAH: So we're out of debate?

LM: I didn't say that.

KAITLYN: What in the City of Sigil is it this time? Aw, come on! What else must I do?

LM: Yes, you've defeated the carron crawlers. Yes, you've survived this incredible fountain battle. Yes, you have failed in your ability to keep your heads down!

LM: Yet suddenly, from high on a grassy knoll out past the shady trees, and the shambling cultists, out past the temple of dragon history, up by the multicolored rosebushes, you see four figures in conversation. One of them is none other than the great Tomithino, who is hunched over, his green dragon hatchling companion clinging to his shoulders. Head bent low, he is conversing with three figures, all of whom are wearing white tanktops, baggy jeans, bright sneaker shoes, and whose necks are loaded with bling.

UTAH: No!

KAITLYN: Dea jay Lazlo?!

SPENCER: And his two beatboys?

LM: The very three. And now The Great Tomithino, who has been alerted to your presence by the commotion at the fountain, points a robed sleeve in your exact direction. And one by one, ever so slowly, the dea jay and his minions turn their brightly blinged necks at the lot of you!

Chapter 11

The Legend of Skay Ting

LM: Did everybody do what they needed to do?

SPENCER: Yeah, but I might still need to talk to a dryad about a brownie at some point. If you know what I mean.

KAITLYN: Unless an egg hatches–

LM: It is getting early.

UTAH: We said we'd go until second sun rise, didn't we? I'm in. Besides, who wants to postpone the celebration that is bound to happen when all Sandy Goans realize we saved the whole city?

SPENCER: And their beer?

LM: Counting your own eggs before they hatch, I see, *Utah*. Well, since everyone is still in, are you all ready for the update? Ok, good. Looks like you've got a narrow escape here, potentially. Let me just see where we left off.

LM: You have been accepted temporarily into a gang of juvenile deleeck wents. They are a lesser-known tribe that is a part of the family tree, but not necessarily always a part of the skay-ter division. They are categorized by their spiky or waist length head hair styles, use of *czar chasm*, *profane comebacks*, and the manner in which they ride their skayte boards on every surface except the sidewalk. As for you, you feel a sense of freedom, power, and adventure riding alongside of them. They are one with the city. One with the streets. They are as a pack of dire wolves roaming the great tundra, searching for things to leap over and howl at, and you are in this pack, running alongside your kin, wind through your coat, tongue lolling out of your–

KAITLYN: Uh, Man Manual says human tongues don't do that with their tongues. Just saying.

LM: Fine. Your tongues are in your mouths. You're racing down along the sidewalks of Bay Park now, a communal set of dwellings within San Deego that overlooks the vast Pass Ifick. And your wheels are spinning underneath you. The leader of the Acolytes of the Hawk howls.

UTAH: Actual Acolytes of the Hawk. Wow. Do they have a toe knee, like the guidebooks say?

LM: Ten toes. Two knees. But no toe knee. All normal.

UTAH: I tell him we're thankful, praise be to Skay Ting.

KAITLYN: Who is Skay Ting?

UTAH: You didn't read the legend of Skay Ting? It was in the last issue of Humans and History. Almost the whole thing was devoted to the skay-ter class. Great scroll on ecology of the deleek went, types of skay-ting boards, skay-ter skills and feats. But the origin story was the best piece I thought.

LM: Well, go ahead and tell it. It's good background that a common human in San Deego would know anyway.

UTAH: Sure. Legend holds that a man known as Skay Ting created the first board when he was being harassed by a foul carron crawler. Seeking safety from the beast, he tried to climb a park tree. He fell out of the tree, bringing the branch of wood he was holding onto with him. As fate would have it, he landed on the board which itself was atop some round decorative beach stones-all of which began to roll as one. He rolled through a human *laundry line*, and all the way down a grassy knoll until he fell into San Deego Bay. When he broke the surface of the water, he not only had escaped his enemy but had also caught a fish for dinner, trapped in between the laundry line and his board. Thus, the board of Skay Ting and the use of human *fishing nets* were invented in the same day.

LM: The deleek-wents clearly appreciate your oral legend and they want to tell you about their own deity, Toe Knee, who they say is a magnificent hawk deity of some kind. However, just as the spiky haired leader of their tribe is about to begin his oral tradition complete with hand gestures and re-enactments, a screeching sound, like that of a thunderous diving roc, erupts behind you. Your human vision is limited, but even so you can make out a streaking yellow wheeled mount, called a *mustang*. No McAdams, its not family like you may think. It is however on fire, large orange and red flames ripping behind the turning wheels. Its aiming just for you! And there's a human inside staring out the window. You can see him now-its Lazlo right there in the clear barrier in the front of human mounts. Sunlight is glinting off the front of the mount, and off his gold teeth wedged between his smiling lips.

UTAH: Is it really on fire?

LM: No. It's a painted illusion. It's not a very good one either.

SPENCER: We're going to be caught! We can't gallop away from this wheeled terror!

LM: Luckily for you, you may not have to. The leader of the deelek-wents turns to you Utah. His eyes are wide. "Dude?" He asks.

UTAH: "Dude," I answer back somberly.

LM: "DUDE!" He points behind you.

UTAH: "Dude!" And I point behind him.

LM: Bruh.

UTAH: Bruh.

LM: Outty.

UTAH: Outty 5000.

LM: That last one was a bit outdated, but he doesn't seem to mind.

UTAH: I embrace the leader with one arm only, and I punch his chest.

LM: He punches yours back.

KAITLYN: This is so freaking beautiful.

UTAH: Run!

SPENCER, KAITLYN: Where?

UTAH: To the building behind us here on the map! The deleek wents are creating a diversion as I speak, one that

Lazlo will not be able to resist. Quick, before Lazlo's passive perception defeats our societal blending modifiers.

KAITLYN: Let's move, people. It's think like a human time.

UTAH: I open the glass door of the building here on the map, the one the deleek went leader told me all about. Behind us, the deleek wents are calling out yo' mama jokes about Lazlo and his mom. There's a screeching of the wheels under the mustang while it tears in an arc away behind me. Everyone in!

LM: The streaking yellow form disappears below the street's horizon line, following the deleek-wents diversionary tactics. You all spill into the building's entrance and fall upon a type of rug that covers the entirety of the space. Success. You've all escaped a dea jay for a second time.

KAITLYN: Its raining reality points people! Woot.

SPENCER: We did it!

KAITLYN: I'm throwing my dust people, just tossing my dust everywhere. You get some dust, and you get some dust, and you get–

LM: Shhhh!!!!

KAITLYN: But I want to–

LM: Shhhhh!!!!

KAITLYN: Why are you doing that? Why does something feel…*literal*?

SPENCER: Wait. Where are we again?

LM: There are various chairs, tables and plants scattered around the space, but by far the most noticeable objects in this temple are the rows upon rows of metallic skeletons stretching from floor to ceiling. These skeletons rise before and around you, bearing heavy loads of incredible treasure. Each structure contains a dozen or more shelves and each shelf is packed with multicolored slabs of faded material.

KAITLYN: Are these…*books*?

LM: There's a smell of old dusty scrolls and the still silence of an empty cave. In the center of the great room is a stone counter, like that of Bart's, only its arranged in a magnificent circle.

KAITLYN: I know what this is!

LM: You're in the lair of a—

KAITLYN, SPENCER, UTAH: Librarian!!!!!

Chapter 12

Lair of the Ancient Silver

LM: You stand frozen in the lair of the most wise and articulate denizen of the real world-a librarian. Your limbs are as petrified as a granite statue in an ancient dwarven ruin. From behind you, a serene, crisp voice punctures the musty air. "Welcome to the Bay Park Library Branch. How can I help you?"

KAITLYN: I. Can't. Look.

SPENCER: Are we dead yet?

UTAH: I'm turning around. Simple as that. If this is the end, then, I will face it with a, "Hello ancient one, we prostrate ourselves—"

LM: "Shhhh!!!!" Hisses the voice. Spicolli, since you are looking, you see no human creature that the voice can belong to, however, in front of you, in pots are two large ferns.

UTAH: I am going to push my literal fear aside and reach out towards the fronds with a single hand-all five fingers.

LM: The frond is not real; it is made of plassed tick.

UTAH: What sacrilege is this?

KAITLYN: Non-real plants in a real world. Only the humans.

LM: As if from the ether, a form appears in the shadow between two of the fronds. Two translucent, intelligent eyes shine behind metal-framed spectacles. To either side of the spectacles, silver chains cascade down and upwards again to wrap behind a protruding neck. Then comes a searching nose, and a thin, pale, skeptical face. The face is wrinkled in places that show a lifetime of consternation and study over old tomes and scrolls. Her face, as well as her entire upper torso, is outlined by waist length silvery hair from the top of her head. Before you, in all her orange-tinted, woolen-scarfed glory, in her abominably animal-printed, sweatered magnificence stands a petite, and ancient librarian.

UTAH: I never thought I'd see the day we–

LM: "You look lost," the ancient one declares. "I am Edna. Perhaps, I can help you find what you seek, today?" Her eyes scan your gear, from McAdams' hill giant hoop to Spicolli's sur-fing board.

KAITLYN: Please don't eat my kitty. Please don't eat my kitty.

UTAH: I prostrate myself before her, close both eyes and put up my tail in a sign of obedience.

LM: That's not possible in human form.

KAITLYN: I attempt to blend into the ferns. Stay quiet, Meyers. Mommy wants to live.

SPENCER: I'm just going to freaking gallop away in any direction at this point.

LM: You're all failing your emotional reactivity saves. Humans are much slower instinctually than we are anyway. Besides, have I asked anyone to roll for initiative?

UTAH: That's never stopped you from bankrupting us before.

LM: Ouch. That hurts socially and emotionally. But seriously, Edna the Wise, like a silvery phantasm, floats betwixt you, and enters a gap in the back of the circular counter. A large sign above it, dangling from the ceiling has large black runes that say, "Help Desk."

LM: "I am very busy today restocking on Tuesdays. So, if you have questions, you'll need to let me know now, please."

SPENCER: This librarian has no apparent plans to academically challenge us? Instead, she offers the wisdom of the ages?

KAITLYN: Thank goodness Edna is a metallic and not a chromatic. Okay, I place one finger to my chin which is a human sign of intense contemplation. Then I ask, "Do you have a treatise on human greetings, by any chance?"

LM: Which language would you prefer, please?

KAITLYN: Uh, how about Chai Knees?

LM: Like a ghost, Edna floats away and disappears between several stacks of old and dusty tomes. In just a few seconds, she drifts back, with an ancient book. Delicately, she places it on the counter before you.

KAITLYN: This is no nightmare, this is a logic-user's dream.

LM: Edna looks at you McAdams. She seems bemused by some of your gear, especially the pool noodle and spongy shield. "And you, Sir?"

SPENCER: Sir? Did you hear that team? By Tanis Half-Elven, she knows a knight when she sees one! "I don't suppose...I don't suppose you have a discourse on human mating rituals and breeding tactics, by any chance?" I make a smile by making my upper lip curl so that my frontal incisors are prominently displayed.

LM: In equal time, she's returned from another section of her library with exactly the treasure you seek.

SPENCER: Lady Chatterley's Lover? Clearly a match for a human knight! But how will I find one woman amongst the entire population?

LM: It's allegorical. Besides, you'll find no greater treasure in this field of study. Let's move on here. The librarian seems either confused, or secretly impressed by your choices thus far. You unfortunately can't tell which. She asks if you are done?

SPENCER: Not even close, m'lady. How about an instrument of proof against documents, by any chance? A scroll of protection +1 versus rhetorical phrases?

LM: Done and done. She brings you the equivalent of both. One tome is entitled, The Firm, by an ancient sage known as John of Castle Grisham. The other is something that humans call *viddy-ohs*, which I am sure you all have read about. This latter one is in a plassed tick box that appears to be a book, but instead houses a strange device inside it. Runes on the front of this small box-like thing read, "A Few Good Men starring Jack Son of a Nickel and Tom's Screws."

SPENCER: Strange.

LM: Indeed. Yet, somehow you sense a percipience of logic within both. Utah?

UTAH: Oh, I don't know. How about a book on kissing other humans, as a human of course? Something about adventure and romance at the same time? You know, just in case that might be coming up.

LM: She seems to examine you carefully this time, as much as she examines the shelves into which she delves. She returns with another book, and another viddy-oh. The book is called The Princess Bride, which strangely features monsters and giants on the front cover. You must be aware that humans are as interested in the fantasy world, as we are of the real world.

UTAH: I've heard that.

LM: Here's the viddy-oh.

UTAH: The 40 Year Old Virgin? What's a virgin I wonder?

KAITLYN: No idea. But congrats. You're going to find out! This is great. How about a dissertation to remove cursed jackets, for McAdams here?

SPENCER: My First Book of– Hi Gene? No idea who Gene is but clearly someone else before me was looking for him too. I'm guessing he must be a great sage who has discovered curse removals. Thank you, Edna the Ancient.

LM: She stares at you unblinking. Peering over her spectacles, she hisses, "Anything else?"

KAITLYN: Yes, ways of the dea jays? Greater or lesser. Or the ecology thereof is okay too.

LM: Most of what she brings you is too difficult to decipher. However, you are able to find one package of scrolls that may hold answers to your inquiries. It's called a *magus zene*. On the cover, runes read "Allee-gee-inda-house, Full List of Quotations."

KAITLYN: This whole library is a treasure trove. I could be here for days.

UTAH: Keep in mind, we don't have days. Just a little while to research. Then we have to be on our way. Only six hours before the file opens.

SPENCER: You're absolutely right Spicolli. I'm going full gallop here. Edna, what do you have about finding clues, seeking treasure and defeating baddies, all while saving entire cities and having the humans admire you?

KAITLYN: Could you throw in some legal stuff?

UTAH: Plus, we'd like to look good while doing it. Just saying…

LM: Edna takes a little longer this time, but she brings you a stack of *viddy-ohs*. "I'm guessing you all don't have time today for Sherlock Holmes. But these should suffice."

LM: You can't make heads, tails, or wings of the titles. But some are at least decipherable: an autobiography of a blonde lawyer and her white wolf-pup familiar, a discourse of powerful human facial expressions by someone who claims to live in the land of zoos, the ace of a place named Ventura, discovered powers of someone called "Austen", and an historical account of raiders of an entity known as the Lost Stark.

UTAH: Its a treasure trove of human insight!

LM: Indeed.

KAITLYN: These are good, but we need something to help us complete our quest in the first place.

UTAH: Right! I know, how about a map with more detail than what Bart gave us. Might save us some time getting to the law firm.

LM: Edna produces something called Thomas' Guide. Even a cursory look through its pages tells you that you can save almost an hour of time due to the fine detailing of this ancient scholar's work!

SPENCER: Sweet nectar!

UTAH: But…that still isn't going to help us stop the devel-lopers. People, we can't just walk into a law firm without any folding money. We'll be bankrupt in no time. Edna, "I need a dissertation on strategies to find money in human civilization?"

SPENCER: And do you have anything to stop a person from spending it on eye scream?

LM: Edna stays put behind the counter this time, and peers at you over her shiny spectacles. She points a bony finger past you, to an entire aisle at your backs. A sign above it reads, "Self-help."

KAITLYN: I get it. Friends, Edna's a powerful librarian, but even her knowledge does not apply to all spheres of logic. Looks like we must split up here a bit, or else we won't have time to peruse everything she gave us.

UTAH: Okay, you all spend some time researching these ancient texts and viddy-ohs separately, while I scan this money-making section. One hour, but no more.

SPENCER: That still gives us 5 hours, which we can do by skayte board. Anyone comes across how to avoid eye scream again, don't keep it to yourselves.

UTAH: Let's do it, team!

* * *

UTAH: Well?

SPENCER: Well, Jacoby and I could only read bits and pieces. Or watch bits on pieces in the crystal box.

UTAH: What's a crystal box?

KAITLYN: It's like a crystal ball, only its shaped like a box. You put the viddy-oh into it and you watch images, like in a crystal ball. Edna taught us all about it. In the *me-dia* room. I know a mage back in our world who would burn his spellbooks for just one of these gadgets.

UTAH: What did you learn from your studies?

KAITLYN: Humans are complicated. But I think we got some great information on how to communicate with humans in tough situations, right McAdams? All in all, it was pretty shagadelic.

SPENCER: All-righty then.

UTAH: Wow. I have no clue what that means, but it sounds great.

KAITLYN: You should have seen it in the crystal box! Extremely powerful. How about you?

UTAH: I am sorry friends. I tried my best. But I failed to find anything that we could use to make quick money. One book said that poor dads can be rich dads, but none of us are human parents. Another book seemed promising. It was about something called flipping. But every time I flipped the book, no money came out. Apparently, in human society you have to have money, before you make money.

LM: Edna leans into your conversation. "Excuse me," she says, "But the Bay Park Library Branch will b e closing in 15 minutes, at 4 pee yam."

UTAH: Uh sorry Edna, I think you mean 3 pee yams.

LM: "No," says Edna who is completely nonplussed about being corrected. "I do mean four pee yam. Perhaps, you've forgotten about day-light savings time?"

KAITLYN: Day light savings–What? What? What in the tower of magus is that?

LM: Sorry friends, Edna is right. None of you took even a single point in human time keeping. Edna is right, you now only have four hours until the file opens. I'm sorry.

UTAH: Now we'll never make it in time, even with the guide of Saint Thomas the Cartographer.

KAITLYN: We have no money for a faster mount.

SPENCER: We're doomed!

LM: "Well, since you surf young man, you could always enter the Mission Beach Surfing Competition

today. Winner earns 50 bucks, which would be plenty of money for a ride anywhere in San Deego. Plus, you get a free membership to the library so I wouldn't charge you when you leave books and viddy-ohs lying around the tables after you're done using them. And it's free to enter, which–" Ancient Edna stops mid-sentence and points to a colorful poster pasted on the window. You missed it when you spilled in because of all the activity going on.

KAITLYN: That's it! Utah, can you do this?

UTAH: I wish to examine the poster, my good Library Master!

LM: Giant waves furl in long rows. A colorful parade of humans is lined up on a beach looking out at the many surfers riding their sur-fing boards. Behind them, palm trees sway in the breeze. Runes read, "Enter the Mission Beach Surfing Competition, March 6th five to six pee yam. All age categories available for entry, men and women. Grand prize 50 dollars." There are images of the winners from last year, for both men and women. The human male who won last year looks like an incredible male specimen. He has bright blue eyes and long blonde hair. He has also suffered significant nose burning, most likely from the sun. His name is Deuce Brockit. But there is also another image on the poster, an image of the female winner.

UTAH: What does she look like?

LM: She is pretty. With large almond brown eyes and brunette hair. She has puffy, kissable lips and fabulously colored mahogany skin. In fact, Utah, she is quite familiar. Its–

UTAH, SPENCER, KAITLYN: Selena??!!!!

*   *   *

LM: Congratulations, you are going at top speed towards Mission Beach. You'll be there any minute. Until then, do you have any questions about the library? I know there was a lot to take in.

KAITLYN: What even was ancient Edna's alignment?

LM: Well, Edna the Wise is an ancient silver. She is the most powerful of the San Deegoan librarians. In fact, she was present when they planted the first branch of the San Deego library. Her alignment is chaotic purposeful. The metallics are a far different type of librarian than your chromatics. Their alignment is almost exclusively chaotic indifferent.

SPENCER: She was wise indeed. Hail to thee, great Edna, she of the many-colored scarf, she of the animal printed sweater vest.

UTAH: Who is ready to take down some devel-lopers?

KAITLYN: Oh I am. I am!

SPENCER: Me too.

LM: Okay, Utah. It's time for you to level up your surfing game.

UTAH: Do you mean–

LM: Unfortunately, friends. I don't mean it *literally*. I was just making a human joke.

UTAH: Snapping turtle! I thought you were serious for a hummingbird's flutter.

LM: You've got a few more reality points to go to make it to level 3.

UTAH: Very funny then.

SPENCER: You know, we've been playing Law Firms and Librarians tonight so long that we're all starting to sound like humans ourselves!

UTAH: Just so long as we don't begin to smell like one, I'm good.

KAITLYN: I'll spread some pixie dust to that! And if I may, I just hope our humble hive of humanity doesn't get destroyed before Utah gets a real shot at a second kiss with Selena.

UTAH: Bankruptcy cannot stop true love, my friend, it can only delay it for a little while.

Chapter 13

Deuce Brockit, the Surf Rocket

LM: "Ladies and Gentlemen below the Surf Broadcast Booth! Welcome back to the 24th annual Mission Beach Surf Competition."

LM: "Val, just look at all these attractive San Deegans on the sand, shopping among the craft vendors, getting ready for sunset and the highlight of the day's events. We expected a large turnout, Val, but it looks to me like there's thousands, not hundreds of sun-blocked spectators down there." A long head-haired human is talking, perfect specimen of a level four surfer class. His nose is blue. Next to him are two other figures. One is a human male, the other a human female.

UTAH: Third level is when you can pick your nose color by the way.

LM: "And they're handsome looking humans!" says the second human male. He too is a surfer-broadcaster hybrid.

SPENCER: Broadcaster is a subclass of dea jay, right? Not a bad build really. Hope we won't have to get into debate with these two.

LM: Correct. He is a twin of the first, but with a green nose.

LM: "Indeed my muchacho. People don't forget to stop by that O'Tavish's wetsuit booth for your lotto ticket. Great prizes. Someone is going to take home this longboard of tranquility behind us here."

LM: "I wish it was me, Val. That's gotta be at least a plus one."

LM: "Plus two, Tyler. Literally takes your action modifier to the next level."

LM: "Wow. Can't wait to see who gets to add that piece of gear to their equipment list. And Val, speaking of winning, have you stopped by the grand champion booth to see the complete prize package?"

LM: "Sick stuff. Year supply of tacos at Taco Surf, this board of tranquility, and let's not forget that chest of 50-dollar bills!"

LM: "Boo yeah! And they all fold, baby."

LM: "Hey, what update can you give the awesome people out there for a surf report? Everyone still prepping for their final competition below is probably too busy gearing up for the tournament's finale right now. But I know they can hear us up here;"

LM: "Good question. We did have an onshore wind kicked up earlier in the afternoon, but with the sunset coming on, the winds are shifting. Flags there on the Big Dipper Roller Coaster behind us are blowing and flapping out towards the sea. As a result, there's a decent shoulder finally appearing over the Santa Bar Bra Street sandbar. But let's check in with the Trisky's Surf Shack official local surf report, Val. You know Trisky's Surf Shack offers more than just great boards and great service. You can stop in any time and get the latest conditions from any of their staff. Why? Because they all surf themselves. Like Trisky here. Trisky, what you got for us?"

LM: "Yo, yo, Tyler. Things are going to get *sick*," says Trisky.

UTAH: Sick is surferese for a fair condition, like when your spring horns grow in just right.

LM: Nice translation, Spicolli. And so you all know, Trisky's a petite human female with dark brown skin and raven colored hair sitting next to Tyler and Val up above you all in the observation deck. "Tide's coming out and that means that nice southwest swell is going to hollow out."

LM: "Sorry Trisky, but all I heard you say was barrels. Just in time too," says Tyler. "Today's final heat is young adult shortboard, and currently there are twelve surfers at the Heat Hut."

LM: "Who do we have this year?" asks Val.

LM: "Definitely a team of regulars Val. Nellie Tator and Don Don Millions are back and either of those two could challenge, of course. But the major talk on the sand today has been the return of the surf rocket, himself."

LM: "Deuce Brockit is back?"

LM: "He sure is Val. And he's clearly added some major surf skill and feats to his already impressive repertoire. I mean, just look at the guy. He's even got a tribal tattoo runed around his upper arm muscle which means he gets a +2 to both his physical attraction modifier and also he has advantage when trying to find a table at local taco shops. If that's not

a level 5 surf athletic build then I don't know what is."

LM: "Tyler, who is that who's been talking to Brockit?"

LM: "Not sure. But rumor has it that there was a last-minute entry to the heat. Here's the roster, ah, yes, thanks Trisky. Guy's name is Utah Spicolli?"

LM: "Did he make that up from a surfer name generator or what?"

UTAH: Hey, I already said I was sorry about that.

LM: "I haven't seen him around Swami's or Cardiff," says Tyler.

LM: "I haven't seen him down by Mission Jetty, Pipes or Scripps either," says Val.

LM: "Guys not a local," says Trisky. "That's for sure."

*   *   *

UTAH: So, I'm standing next to Deuce now? Ok, cool. And Spencer and Kaitlyn are walking the shops behind me looking for any clues I might need. And for…

LM: Selena. Yep. But they haven't seen her yet, lover boy. So, hold your hill giants.

UTAH: What's the surf rocket like, anyway?

LM: Up close you can tell that he really is a fine surf specimen. His chest looks like it was chiseled from sandstone. Even with his feet in the water up to his ankles, he is a full head taller than you, Utah. His shaggy sand-colored hair not only helps him to camouflage with his surroundings, but it also moves water down towards his back. Sea water dribbles from the impressive sea-lion mane slicked over his head, leaving his hawkeyes to scan the sea. With vision that few humans can achieve, he finds every white cap, every crest.

KAITLYN: Are his fingers and toes webbed, like my cousin Nettie the Nymph?

LM: No, humans cannot change their bodies because of magic spells or a witch's curse like what happened to Nettie when she caught that old hag skinny dipping. They need a type of ointment, something called *evah lotion*. It is a very dangerous substance, requiring legendary alchemical prowess. Takes generations to make. But you get the sense that Deuce doesn't need evah lotion. Even with your pathetic human senses, you can smell the sea on him. In his massive hands, his board is covered in colorful runes and images of various sizes and shapes.

UTAH: That means *sponsoring*, just so every human knows. Lots of folding dollars and logical items.

LM: Right! And sponsoring from a local merchant peddling a logical product called wax of sexing. That's how Deuce is now holding a short board of shredding, +3. He helps the merchant sell their wax of sexing.

UTAH: Oh behave!

SPENCER: Is that like a wax to rub on a human in order to determine gender? Because that would be helpful.

LM: Not quite McAdams. But as Utah knows, surfers put wax on their board, giving them a plus four to righteously air, pull a floater or drop-in on a gnarly barrel.

UTAH: Maybe Deuce has sex with it? It is a plus three! I would.

LM: He's also wearing a wetsuit of warmth. It would make that difficult.

UTAH: He's my idol. I'm his zealot.

LM: Deuce is what humans call *legit*. For example, each muscle is sculpted into a perfect functional shape, like a…well…a unicorn's front and hind quarters.

SPENCER: Thank you.

LM: You're welcome.

UTAH: What does the rest of the competition look like?

LM: There's not much else in terms of competition, Utah. As you're about to find out.

UTAH: Watcha mean?

LM: Deuce switches his board to his right hand with swift precision, then he places his left hand on your shoulder, squeezing it firmly with his five fingers.

KAITLYN: Oh dear. That's a sign of patronization, it's a rhetorical pre-debate action!

UTAH: What the swamp does Jacoby mean?

LM: It means that Deuce is already making the match unbalanced. You've now got a -2 to your male ego. I hope I don't need to remind anybody here that human male egos are particularly fragile in moments of contestation with other potential breeding males.

LM: "Nice board, brah," says Deuce completing the ritual. "Where'd you get that hunk of balsa wood from? A thrift store in the *vallllley?*"

UTAH: Swamprats!

LM: Utah, you've been hit with a type of verbal assault known as a *roast*. We went over this in that mini-adventure I hosted a few moons ago called,

Smack Down in Teenage Town. Either give a comeback or you've got another -2 to your ego.

KAITLYN: Ouch, a czar chasm daily. This guy is a pro.

UTAH: I could make fun of his hairless torso. His tiny ears? Uncloven feet? I got nothing people.

SPENCER: Sorry Utah. We're shopping in another part of the beach so technically we don't even hear any of this.

LM: Correct. Utah, you are on your own here. Or are you? Suddenly, there's a shuffling of feet moving through the sand behind you. Then, a voice. Its familiar. Female.

LM: "Hey Brockit. Utah here may have bought his board in the valley, but at least he doesn't wait for a sponsor to pay him to get stoked. Why don't you head back to the Heat Hut and rub some sex wax all over yourself. Maybe you'll finally get mounted."

LM: Before you, Deuce's mouth drops open. If you guessed this is a high-level roast, you guessed right! Brocket quickly recovers and brings his jaws back together again. He seems as though he is about to consider another verbal assault, but then without another word, he shakes his head and shambles back to the tent known as the Heat Hut. You, Mr. Spicolli, thanks to your surprise savior have gained back *all* of your ego points.

UTAH: Epic!

SPENCER: I wish I could have been there to try my own roast. It's like the one thing this jacket—

UTAH: Where is my champion? I swear fealty m'lord!

LM: You spin around Utah, and stare into the human face of none other than she of your first kiss she of the chestnut hair locks, and the large doe eyes.

KAITLYN: Sweet springtime honey!

SPENCER: Mountain meadows!

UTAH: Selena!

LM: But she's far more divine than when you saw her last. Now she is in her element. Surfboard in hand, hair slicked back by the sea water, covered in a wetsuited armor that gives a +3 versus cold, +5 when she urinates inside of it, which she indeed does. She is a goddess before you Utah. A human surf goddess.

UTAH: What in the Feywild do I do with a divine goddess lubricated in her own urine? Should I try and kiss her again? I'm so confused.

LM: "Sup Utah," says Selena. She raises her chin slightly. "Deuce was always a butthole. Surfer, sure, but a butthole more."

SPENCER: What is a butthole surfer?

KAITLYN: No idea. But this is fascinating.

LM: "Ever since I went on a date with that creep, he's been so competitive. He always has to be the big *kah huna* everywhere he goes. Ride the primo waves. But Utah," says Selena. She pauses momentarily to take one of your hands in one of her hands. This increases your male ego by one, "You're so totally chill how you just stood there. Like you didn't even care. So laid back. Any chance we can be he lua?"

UTAH: Is this a question?

LM: Yes, it is. What do you say?

UTAH: I point my finger right at her... nose? Then I say, "Yeah baby, yeah."

LM: "You really are a nut Utah, you know that?" Selena then plants a kiss upon your cheek, giving you one final +1 to ego. She whispers, "Go beat him out there, surfer *guy*."

SPENCER: Wait. Selena was The Rocket's mate for breeding at some point? Are there offspring? Because that would make a great sequel if we had to fight their henchmen offsprin–

UTAH: "Selena," I say. "I'm going to show you surfing like you've never seen it before." Then, I pucker my lips like last time, and slam my upper jaw right into hers.

KAITLYN: Oh, this is just so romantic. I wish I could spread dust all over you both right now.

          *   *   *

LM: "Val, do you think Don Don's got a legitimate shot this year. Does he look like he's fully recovered from his reef injury?"

LM: "Well, he paddled out pretty solid Ty, but what I think most people on the sand still want to know is why the hell did Utah just headbutt Selena Dominguez? I mean is there some kind of love triangle with The Rocket we don't know about?"

LM: Good news there, Val. Selena's being examined by an *ee ham tee* over in the first aid hut. Reports are that she wasn't unconscious for very long.

LM: That's great to hear that she'll make a full recovery.

LM: Let's get back to the action. As you know all twelve contestants in the final heat have moved into position just past the breakers. We've got The Rocket in red of course and Don Don Millions in green. Nellie Taylor in blue and his brother Swellie in orange. But where's the new guy? Wasn't he in–

LM: There Val! Utah's drawing first blood again, but this time in the water! Check out his streaking yellow chested human shaped form whizzing down the face of that monstrous wave! Clearly the biggest set of the heat so far. Like woah. Dude, that wave has got the best barrel, bro. He's taking off! Now, pulling in, crouching down like a springing displacer beast. Utah's charging down the face of that wave which can only be described as a water elemental being conjured by a high level sorcerer!

KAITLYN: I can so picture this.

LM: Boom! He's gone Ty. The wave swallowed him up. Wipe out!

LM: No. No. Listen to the crowd below. There! He's been spit out! Smacking the lip. Whaback! Smacking the lip. Whaback! He's dropping back down, and holy smokes muchachos. He's pitted!

LM: So pitted, Ty!

SPENCER: I do not understand any of that.

LM: It's surferese. Surfers get very animated when describing their endeavors. It's sort of like a fawn in a flute-maker's shop.

UTAH: Oh man and that is just the best time ever.

LM: Quiet you. Now let's all not get too meta on the magical metaphors-they're there just to give you a

taste of the real world. Besides…Spicolli, you're in the barrel! Utah's first wave of the competition is impressive. Getting barreled and spat out is the ultimate ride for surfers. Judges' score cards are up at the judge's table-Think of it like a knight's tournament. Utah's average is 9 out of 10. He's now the surfer to beat.

UTAH: Yes!

KAITLYN: Breeze yeah, Spicolli! Even though you can't hear me with your sad human ears on the beach!

LM: Just listen to that crowd Val. They're going dire hogs for truffles down on the sand. Huge crowd formed at the water's edge clapping their two hands together for Spicolli. Never seen anything like it.

LM: Got some interesting folks here today, Ty.

LM: No doubt.

LM: Trisky, What's up with that lady earlier who had the orange cat on her head. I heard her asking about "legal surf parameters"? She said she was Spicolli's "surf legal assistant." Is this something new with a sponsor we haven't heard about?

LM: I don't know Val. Maybe we can ask her. And check it out, she's right down in front by the water's edge. That cat is still on her head, scratching her face all up. Damn thing is trying to hold on for dear life so it doesn't fall in the sea.

KAITLYN: Cats hate water in San Deego too?

LM: Yep.

KAITLYN: Uh, oh. Sorry Meyers.

LM: Dude, Next to Cat Lady is that other strange fella. Dude was straight up strutting with a pool noodle and boogie board like he was a knight and they were some kind of sword and shield.

SPENCER: Well, duh.

LM: "Guys!" Whispers Trisky. "Your mic is still on."

LM: Oh, uh hmmm…okay folks, back to the action here. Today's final heat is brought to you by Trisky's Surf Shack. Trisky's Surf Shack, where real surfers go to get real surf gear and updates. Not bogus stuff like in the valley.

LM: Ty, looks like another set is coming in. The crowd sees it too, many cheers. Spicolli and Deuce are both paddling hard for the crest. They're turned. Both gunning for it. This may decide the entire match right here!

* * *

UTAH: Okay my fae friends, prepare thyselves for my ultimate adventure moment! I am about to turn this skill challenge upside down and surf right into level three.

LM: You might wish to pay attention, Spicolli. You've got a massive set of waves rolling in. Biggest of the session so far, and biggest of the day. You'll need a set of very good rolls, not just for catching the waves, but you'll need to beat Brocket's board of shredding modifier for take-off.

UTAH: Not a problem, amigo. I've been kissed by Selena, and my ego is *swole!* I have…wait for it…a 19 for takeoff! As a surfer I get *stokage* on 19 or 20. Sweet honeydew nectar! Now, I'm paddling into position with a…raw sixteen…for wave position and a fourteen for surf style. *Cowabun—*

LM: That's not bad, but Deuce…I'm sad to report to you…just rolled an 18.

SPENCER: *Neiiiiiiigh.*

KAITLYN: Oh deer.

LM: Modified of course by both his logical board and his human machismo index. It's a feat for surfers available at level 7. Take note there Utah.

KAITLYN: Brockit's a level 7! Dear deer.

UTAH: Doesn't matter. I kissed a girl yesterday. So now, I'm paddling right next to him, using my swole stokage. Gonna both try and intimidate him and bluff the takeoff.

LM: You must pick one since he's more than 4 levels your senior.

UTAH: Bluff, then.

LM: Sadly, that was the wrong answer. Deuce will now use an automatic lair action, since he's local here. With a quick glance back at the beach for positioning, he pulls into the breaking crest of the wave. Surfer's call this the *sweet spot*. He knows right where the wave breaks on this beach better than anyone, and because he is nearer to where the wave is breaking, he also has the right of way. Sadly for you, he also has the right to any points from surfing this very wave. And my human friends, it's a monster. As tall as the dragon head of a chimera, as quick as a cave fisher's tongue, and as powerful as a storm giant's fury. Brocket is about to ride the wave of his life. And you, Spicolli, are in his way. You'll need to pull your board back now, or risk disqualification from the contest. You'll most likely also be *haws-spitalized,* and *bank-ruptured* as a result. If you survive the wipeout that is.

UTAH: Well, I'm still taking off. You hear that beach people. Utah Spicolli, level 2 human surfer, is taking off anyway!

LM: You're what?

KAITLYN: Moonbeams and mushrooms!

UTAH: Do or cyclops eye, that's my motto. If I'm going down in a wave of glory, I'm taking someone down with me. I'm not letting this human–

LM: You forgot that the rocket is immune to your bluff while in the water for a full day. He's in full human male glory, shredding the wave to pieces. This is going to not only net him the victory but could entice Selena to consider him once more as a breeding partner. A surfer's prowess can be more of an aphrodisiac than the powdered liver of an ettercap.

SPENCER: Pixie powder! We were so close on this one.

LM: Deuce just needs to make one more roll and so long as it isn't a–

UTAH: Library master, I beg thee of only one more thing. Will you describe my death scene? I've never died as a human surfer before.

KAITLYN: You deserve this death, you know that?

UTAH: Remember to loot my body everyone.

*   *   *

KAITLYN: So how did Utah give up his roast?

SPENCER: I'm pretty sure it's 'give up the toast'. Hipsters love toast, so I would know. And what did you roll for Deuce's wave because anything other than a critical mi–

LM: Ty stands. Val stands. "Ladies and gentlemen of the surfing world. I simply do not believe what my eyes have been witness to here today! There is pandemonium on the sand. There is pandemonium up here in the broadcast booth."

LM: I think even the fish are freaking out Ty!

LM: No doubt. This is stokage on a massive scale my friends. Let's send it down to Trisky at the shoreline. Somebody is about to be greeted with a huge cache of cash.

LM: Val says, "Not to mention the logical items that goes with the winner's purse."

LM: Ty says, "And the permanent boost to their attraction modifier."

LM: Val says, "Now, sending it live to Trisky with the interview the beach has been waiting for!"

KAITLYN: Oh my god, is it Utah?

SPENCER: I'd almost bet my horn it's Utah!

KAITLYN: Everyone, what do I always say? Say it with me.

KAITLYN, SPENCER, UTAH, LM: Never bet wings or horn, especially fae and unicorns.

LM: I'm going to skip over a part here, but I promise we'll come back to it.

UTAH: Hardly seems fair.

LM: A huge crowd is gathered around a stage constructed for the purpose of showcasing the winners of the surfing tournament. Various young humans of different sizes are standing proudly in a line. Before each of them is a magnificent trophy which appears to be made of solid gold, and intricately shows a surfer riding a huge wave. The winners of the tournament all wear flowers that have been cut off at their stems, and placed one after the other on a string that wraps around their necks, dangling in the front of their chests like an orc's ear necklace.

KAITLYN: The villains!

LM: At the end of the line stands our Grand Champion. Trisky is there, holding the mic, which is something in her hands that logically enchants a voice to become louder. She asks, "So Deuce, was

there ever a moment when you thought you wouldn't win?"

SPENCER: Nooooooo!

LM: Deuce holds up the surfing trophy that Ty and Val have just handed him. All around the platform stands the horde of human spectators. Their arms are pumping in the air. All are chanting in unison like acolytes in a temple, or some magical spell, "Rocket! Rocket! Rocket!"

LM: Deuce says, "Hang on, let me put this little guy down here." He then, takes you Spicolli off his muscled bronzed shoulders. He sets you feet first onto the beach."

UTAH: Where I stand up on my unhoofed legs and—

LM: Actually you fall over on your unhoofed legs, face first into the sand. Deuce then continues while you wail into the salty grains, "Well, you see, there's been some talk that it was going to be somehow impossible for The Rocket to do what no other San Deego surfer has ever done-take a sixth Mission Beach Surf Trophy home." This announcement elicits shouts of "No way!" and more chants of "Rocket" from the crowd. "That's six, consecutive, mind you. But," continues Deuce and he holds up his trophy. Then, he cups a hand to his puny human ear. "But were those rumors true?"

SPENCER: Unless you roll a six, they never are, are they?

KAITLYN: Not a bad idea about cupping the ears. We should try this!

LM: The crowd roars his name! Deuce laughs, "As you can hear, the rumors of my surf demise have been greatly exaggerated."

LM: Trisky exhales a compliment, "Wow Deuce, such stokage, on such a scale, on such a stage. But I think what everyone wants to know, is just what exactly happened on that last wave!"

UTAH: Yeah, that would be nice.

LM: Deuce breathes in deeply, "It went down like this, Trisky my dear. You see that little valley poser on the sand? The guy calling himself Utah Freaking Spicolli?" This further elicits quite a united laugh from the crowd.

UTAH: "Uh, that's just Utah Spicolli, thank you," I say.

LM: Quiet, you can barely exhale at this moment. "That little guy full-on tried to drop-in on me!" The crowd's laughter becomes a collective gasp amongst the crowd. Ty and Val actually take a step backwards.

LM: Trisky screeches, "Bro, no way!"

LM: Deuce answers, "Yes way, Trisky. Yes way. I was pulling in, deep into the barrel, when I look over the lip and see someone trying to snake my ride. So, I was like, no way. No one drops in on Deuce Brockit, Surf Rocket."

LM: "And then?" Trisky prompts. Her eyes are wide like a doe's.

LM: The crowd falls into a hushed silence. Deuce has clearly been waiting for this moment. "Well then you must have all seen it because it was sick! Ha ha! But for those who couldn't because of bad human eyesight let me recount it for you footstep by footstep. You see when I saw the poser coming up over the wave's lip, I thought it would be a double wipe-out. But then, I used reserved stokage to roll up above him, just as he was being slammed down into the white water."

LM: Trisky gasps, "You used Spicolli as a human water shield?"

LM: "Sure did Trisk. And before my eyes, there he is flying over the falls, slammed headfirst into his own board."

UTAH: Wait. What?

LM: "Which broke it in half, if I'm not correct?" Says Trisky. Next to her, an assistant holds up the two pieces to the crowd. Once they are placed side by side, any monster can clearly see the defined outline of Utah's exact human face. People buzz over this new information. "And then," continues Deuce, "that's when I knew this was more than a heat, people. I had to save this little poser, because you know, not only am I the best surfer in Mission Beach, but I have a heart, too."

KAITLYN: Well so do—wait, do we?

SPENCER: Deuce is just so dreamy.

LM: "I grabbed this little dork by the back of his pantaloons, then, threw him over my shoulder, executed a perfect floater off the lip, as you all saw, and dropped back into my post-barrel spit out stance. That's when the wave spat me out, and you all saw the rest."

SPENCER: I think I now understand how that aboleth down in Sparier collected all those thralls.

KAITLYN: Or when that wilderness wraith turned that one adventuring party into ghouls with just his aura. Remember?

LM: "We sure did, didn't we crowd?" Trisky says grinning from one ear to the other. "The first double barrel, single tandom board wave in Mission Beach heat history!" She stands and pumps her fist towards Deuce, while around the platform others do the same. They chant, "Rocket! Rocket! Rocket!" It is now just you three, behind the backs of the crowd. You can see through the many outstretched arms, that Deuce is

lifting his trophy high above it all. Unfortunately, Spicolli, you will not be earning anything as you were disqualified once your board was broken.

UTAH: Man Manual says that my face will become very red right now. And that I will feel something called *hatred* towards Deuce? What is hatred? First, let me just tell Deuce that I am so glad he saved me. Of course, we needed to win the purse to save the whole town but his reputation is also rather important. Just let him know that his extra labors were greatly appreci—

KAITLYN: Utah, humans do not react the way we fae folk do. Come on, you know that.

SPENCER: Got it. Right here, page 324. Says you are experiencing *shame* as well, Utah. In fact, massive amounts of shame.

UTAH: An attack?

SPENCER: Nope. Just a human characteristic. From what I once heard from an elf it's like twilight in the meadow when your flute snaps a string.

UTAH: Wouldn't I just ask for another?

KAITLYN: Or when you flit onto a perfectly sun-kissed perch and slip into a leaf pool.

UTAH: Well, I don't really get it. But I'll do my best to roleplay!

KAITLYN: More importantly is that we didn't win that treasure purse, did we? So now all we have is these two boards of skay ting to try and get us to the lair on time. We already know we can't make it. So—

LM: The pulsing crowd is dancing and swaying around Deuce. Except for one lone figure, which is Selena. She emerges through the pack, and walks towards you. Her face is sympathetic.

UTAH: Well, I get that one.

LM: She is carrying a satchel over her back and has something shiny in her hands.

KAITLYN: What are they? Tokens of defeat?

LM: They are keys on a golden ring. "I'd love to stick around and hear more of Deuce's gloating, but...Come on, Utah. Let's get you home. Something tells me you and your friends do not have a *karr*. I'll take you wherever you need to go."

SPENCER: What's a karr?

LM: It's what humans call small versions of their wheeled mounts.

UTAH: Wait, Selena has one of these? And she is its master?

KAITLYN: Enchanted keys of destiny!

SPENCER: We're not out of this one yet!!!!

Chapter 14

A Billion Deaths Served

LM: For the last time, you feel no wind unless you stick your head out of the window. And for the last time, if you stick your head out of the window, then you might get it cut off by a passing karr going the opposite direction.

UTAH: I really think these wheeled mounts are overrated. What's the point of riding a mount if you don't have wind through your horns?

KAITLYN: You've got to get real, Utah. As humans, we must forget misty breezes and flower fragranced twilights. All we care about right now is that we're going to make it to the file on time. We have a *real* chance to stop it from opening thanks to Selena, here. Isn't that right?

LM: It is. Currently, you find yourselves racing down the human roads thanks to the wheels under this karr, speeding towards the lair of the devel-lopers, known to you only as Minick and Minick. Selena has a logical item called a watch which she wears on her wrist like jewelry. It apparently tells her telepathically that there are currently more than eight pee yams.

KAITLYN: Woah.

LM: It's like a sun-dial but speaks to her even after sunset. It is telling her that you will just make it before nine pee yams. But there is no time to spare. Selena is behind a gigantic wheel, which she turns one way and the other making this beast you now ride within do her bidding. She talks over her shoulder to you all. You are seated side by side on a type of soft log designed to cushion your two buttocks behind her. "So, let me get this straight," she says. "You lot rode boards of skay-ting, who was a dude, all the way from Bahl Boa Park to Mission Beach. Utah then entered the surf contest so that you could win prize money which you wanted just to pay for a ride to what you call a devel-loper lair."

SPENCER: Not a bad summary. But you forgot the stockpile of logical items we hoped to acquire which would give us an advantage during the final battle, surely soon to come.

Utah: We still plan to logic load before the BBEG, right?

LM: "And," Selena continues, "You believe that the people inhabiting this so-called lair, are making nefarious plans about the Tiki Mermaid at this very moment. In less than one hour, their evil plan will come to fruition-unless you stop the file from 'opening'. This then necessitates a large-scale battle which you plan to commence upon arrival to the law firm, er, I mean, lair of the—

KAITLYN: Evil doers. Yes, that is right. Wow. I mean, she really is a surfing goddess and has quite the memory, as well.

LM: "And, if we don't stop the file from opening, er, the file of dread, from opening, foul things will be loosed upon the city of San Deego. All will be…"

SPENCER: "Lost. All will be lost."

LM: Selena nods and smiles sweetly. "And can you all tell me why I shouldn't stop first at the police station?"

UTAH: Oh, dear one. That's a lovely idea to collect some henchmen for our cause, but right now there are just no more pee yams for such things.

LM: Selena just nods up and down. A sign she understands. Do you want me to describe the journey or can we skip ahead a bit?

UTAH: I think we get the sniff.

LM: There are no random encounters along the way, unless you count a particularly clever carron crawler who slow-marched across the road in front of you.

SPENCER: Alone?

LM: Yes.

UTAH: Ambush?

LM: Not likely. Carron crawlers use something called an *elitist stare* when they sense oncoming danger. This was simply a non-debate immediate reaction. The stare is what slowed your mount's wheels, allowing her to walk across the road unimpeded.

KAITLYN: Ghastly.

LM: Like a veil pulled over the sky, night descends on San Deego's Lah Hoya community of nobles. In case you haven't gotten to that part of the Merry Can Setting and Campaign Guide, Merry Cans like to separate their towns and hamlets by wealth. This particular area is partitioned by thickly grown hedges for only the nobles of the city.

UTAH: Like royalty?

LM: No, not quite. In fact, the only factor in their noble status is an extraordinarily powerful item, which they must yearly fight to keep. In springtime, each adult human in the area is given something called a *neighbor's hood*. This hood is the source of all of their social power. They will then enter a deadly arena, and battle a foul demon known as Tackz Uz.

KAITLYN: I have heard of the fiend!

LM: Indeed. Humans are very fearful of Tackz Uz, almost as much as death itself. Each will need to survive for a while in the arena, until the demon's blood rage is appeased. If the human is successful, he may continue to live in his noble home for one more year. If they are not, it's basically a total party bill, and he is stripped of the neighbor's hood and the power that comes with it.

UTAH: Poor Lah Joyans. Can you imagine the worry?

LM: Humans call it *stress*. Whole chapter in Man Manual.

SPENCER: No thanks. The only thing I need to battle in the meadow is a rock or two when I lay my head down to sleep.

UTAH: Sometimes a very inquisitive firefly, but otherwise…

LM: Just then, the karr comes to a halt. Staring through the window, your gaze floats upward along the impressive façade of the most magnificent fortress you have seen in San Deego. The moon outlines its enormous and imposing girth. It is many humans tall, perhaps thirty or more. You can almost imagine two gigantic arms breaking free of the stone from either side and reaching out to grab you for a meal. The building is mostly constructed of glass and stone, but none of the windows are candlelit-save two. Your gaze drifts to the very top of the building, where two glowing lights, like golden snake's eyes, stare down at you menacingly. Above them, a sign, illuminated by the moon and starlight, glows ominously: *The Law Firm of Minick and Minick.*

LM: "We've arrived just in time," says Selena. "Inside that building is the file you dread. And something tells me, the devel-lopers guarding it aren't going to be surprised you're coming."

*   *   *

UTAH: So we're in something called a *lobby*?

LM: Yes.

UTAH: And the main doors just happened to be open to the entire fortress?

LM: Building. Yes.

KAITLYN: And just clarifying, but there was no moat?

LM: No moat.

SPENCER: And so far, no traps?

LM: No.

UTAH: And we either can take stairs upwards which will weaken us physically or attempt to use a device known as an *elf hater*. Any ideas why it hates elves?

LM: Supposedly, Law Firms and Librarians is releasing a Tome of Logic in the spring and rumors have it the elf hater will be explained there. But basically, yes, those appear to be your choices. Selena informs you that her watch has given her an update. You now have only *men its*, not pee yams. They are shorter. And you are down to just ten of them.

UTAH: I don't like this time crunch. Let's pool our resources like we did that one time in Lost Ambulance. That's it, just dump everything here on the floor of the lobby. We'll load up, and take the elf-hater?

KAITLYN: Humans and History says the risk of an elf hater trapping a human is quite small.

SPENCER: Utah, what are you going to do about Selena?

KAITLYN: She isn't ready for this level of debate, lover boy.

UTAH: I know. I've been thinking about how to tell her because I think she'd sacrifice herself for me financially. Okay, I take Selena by the shoulders and pull her towards my face.

LM: She instinctively shields her face with her hands.

KAITLYN: Love is so cute.

UTAH: "Selena," I tell her, "There is something I have to tell you. Something that is going to be very hard for you to understand. You see, when I first came here, you thought I was a human surfer. And—

LM: "I'm just going to go wait in the karr," says Selena. "You kids have fun up there. Try and keep it under an hour please. I've got work in the morning." She then pushes a small round button near the elf hater behind you, and walks out of the lobby, and back to her mount.

KAITLYN: Gods, what a stoic!

SPENCER: Alright, then. This is the way it should be, just us three. I couldn't picture us sending in the non-player human as a shield anyway. Not Selena. Let's load up. I'm going to take off my dea jay's jacket and instead—

LM: Nice try. But you know that thing isn't coming off until you appease its curse.

SPENCER: Fine. Fine. Then, I'd like to chug all seven potions of monster energy.

LM: At the same time?

SPENCER: Sure. Their effects stack right?

LM: Maybe. You don't know.

SPENCER: Down the gullet they go!

LM: Okay. Anyone else want to logic-load?

UTAH: Well, I'm bringing my board of sur-fing of course. But I think I'll also bring that hoop of hill giant hula.

LM: You are aware that you have no free hands?

UTAH: Isn't that when humans say we use our heads?

LM: True but remember that you only have one of those.

UTAH: Understood. Kaitlyn, what about you?

KAITLYN: I'm keeping my hands free. Just Meyers coming with me here in his backpack.

LM: Okay. Let me find this next part…I've been wanting to read this for moons! Here we go: Standing

in the law firm lobby, a single beam of moonlight shining down upon you from the night sky through the glass, you have never felt more human, more logical. The goodly folk of an entire city depend on you, and that fills you with hope. You know what you must do, and now is the time to do it. Behind you, a small noise chimes, breaking the moment of contemplation. The elf hater's portal, like a dragon's gaping maw, opens sideways. Inside, is revealed an empty metallic box capable of swallowing you all whole.

UTAH: Shall we enter the giant open mouth of destiny?

LM: If I had a gold coin for every time you lot have said that I'd be a rich ogr—

KAITLYN: Since this is the finale, would it be okay to check on the tadpoles first? I promised a bullfrog I would.

SPENCER: I really ought to prance a bit before we're too committed here.

LM: Fine. Fine. Just so we're all decided to finish this out tonight, right?

UTAH, SPENCER, KAITLYN: Yeah, baby. Yeah!

*   *   *

LM: I'm so sorry about tadpole 4519. But you really can't blame yourself. Every pixie has to—

KAITLYN: I'm a big fae. Really. You can continue now, Master of Reality.

LM: Library Master, please. Okay, all. Let's get back to the action! After the portal closed, you felt a strange sensation in your stomach.

UTAH: Like when your fae friends flip you around during a twilight prance?

KAITLYN: Like when you flutter amongst the falling fall leaves?

LM: Something like that. But the point is that—

SPENCER: I think it's so weird how real portals make your stomach feel the same as magical portals do. Don't you all?

LM: Hush. This is why I swamp ruled break time moons ago. Any more than a dozen dewdrops and you people lose focus.

UTAH: He called us people, again!

LM: (intelligible grunting noise, followed by the sound of scroll paper unrolling) The elf hater's jaws open wide, to reveal a dark and foreboding corridor, the end of which is obscured by darkness. We've

already debriefed about your sad human eyesight in darkness so no comments here please. Along both sides of the corridor, arranged every full gallop or so, or ten wing flutters if you will, stand carved pedestals, with a flat surface. On each surface rests various shapes, which you can't quite see yet. From somewhere far away, you hear a peaceful sound-of music, from many instruments. With the music, there is a sad yet melodious female voice singing in Eng Lish. The words are vague, but the voice is so real, so genuine, that you find your head bobbing along with the rhythm.

UTAH: I try to stop it.

LM: You cannot.

KAITLYN: Do we want our heads bobbing to this rhythm?

LM: Yes, you do. All humans do. McAdams really likes it. Don't you McAdams?

SPENCER: "Yes, I do", I say and lovingly pet my jacket not knowing why.

UTAH: I will cautiously, inhumanely as possible, creep towards the first pedestal and observe the first shape resting upon it with whatever vision I can muster.

LM: Resting atop the first pedestal is a yellow and red castle. Runes in Eng Lish read: Mack Donald's. Under this sign is another, much smaller set of runes

which you can just make out. They read, "Over one billion served."

UTAH: Served what?

LM: You aren't sure.

UTAH: I call for the others. Spencer, Kaitlyn, what is this madness? A home for little animals?

LM: No. Humans enjoy building small versions of larger things. They call them *models*. This is a model of something much larger, which the devel-lopers built.

UTAH: And then they served death to over 1 billion other humans within it's foul red and yellow walls no doubt.

KAITLYN: I'd like to *detect illegal*. It's an at-will.

LM: You're getting mixed readings, Jacoby. Almost as if something is–

KAITLYN: Blocking it?

LM: Correct. And back to you Utah. Behind the model, now that your eyes are adjusting to what little light exists in the corridor, you see a human *pho-toe*. There is a small meadow, with flowering bushes, trees and grasses-no doubt home to some peaceful creatures and insects. A creepy human dressed in red and yellow, with white war paint splashed across his

face, glares excitedly at you. He holds a large sign that features two successive yellow arches. Underneath that in Eng Lish, are words: Coming Soon to serve you! Mack Donald's.

KAITLYN: Unholy union of darkness and despair!

SPENCER: It's far worse than we thought. Obviously, these devel-lopers have let loose this foul demon, no doubt their conjurations were the result of their ignorant hubris. This once peaceful glade has now been destroyed for this unholy temple.

UTAH: Where one billion human souls have been sequestered. Our enemies must be powerful indeed to summon such a fiend as this…Mack Donald!

LM: Do you wish to view the others?

UTAH: Oh deer.

LM: Walking along the corridor, each step brings you closer to a certain feeling of impending doom. Every pedestal is adorned by a small, yet imposing model of some fortress, castle, or another hopeless bastion of evil. Behind each, like skeletons in a dragon's lair, lie photos of what the devel-lopers have proudly annihilated: majestic hills of cascading grasses, sun-kissed meadows of flowering meadows, and seaside beaches, where waves gently washed ashore. But now, in a sad state of reality, each has been polymorphed into the aberration before you. Your only sad reprieve is that you do not have to look upon the true scale of the abominable structures. Yet, even in miniature, there are many fortress complexes, which you may refer to in Humans and History as *mahls*.

UTAH: Missed this. What's a mahl?

LM: This monstrosity is long, wide, more than a dozen humans tall, and contains countless doorways to incalculable shame. In this accursed place, humans do something call *shop until you drop*.

SPENCER: Imagine the pain.

LM: Indeed. There is another temple to Mack Donald-the demon's likeness again appearing to dance. His maniacally smiling face is clearly boasting about the souls he has taken. But the largest of all of the models is one that halflings even the mahl.

UTAH: Pray tell what foul name is enshrined upon it?

LM: It reads, "Wall Mart."

KAITLYN: Wall Mart? Where you go to buy walls?

LM: Not quite.

SPENCER: Does this enormous temple feature a demon mocking the once peaceful space it destroyed, too?

LM: No. But this model is very detailed. When you look closely, you can see many small humans exiting

the temple, pushing a type of wheeled cart towards their mounts.

UTAH: What's in the carts?

LM: You can't tell, there are many objects of various sizes and shapes, all hidden in bags, and in chests.

SPENCER: Clearly this Wall Mart demon is not collecting souls but is instead using acolytes to spread his demon spawn in the nearby community!

UTAH: I think we all see that too, McAdams.

KAITLYN: These devel-lopers are fiends beyond comparison!

UTAH: They must be stopped, regardless of what happens to us tonight. Agreed?

SPENCER, KAITLYN: Agreed.

LM: You have arrived at the end of the corridor, to the very end of the corridor, where a vast double door rests against the wall. Under the door, you can make out the source of the music, but still not the words of the sonorous enchantress singing. Here too lies the last of the pedestals. Like a hive of bees, your heads are swirling with what you have seen. And as a decaying log, you feel hollow at the wanton destruction of so much beauty the humans would have otherwise enjoyed. But now you see that the last pedestal's top does not hold a model. Behind the

vacant pedestal hangs a pho toe of none other than the Tiki Mermaid. In the background of the picture is the San Deego Bay sprawling off into the horizon. It's waters shimmer in the fading sun.

KAITLYN: They must not touch our beloved alehouse.

UTAH: I have never been more ready for a BBEG.

SPENCER: They aren't going to get away with any more mahls, any more marts of walls. The Mack Donald himself can feel my noodle of poodling upon his war-painted brow! This law firm isn't serving any more deaths on my watch-not so long as I have breath in my lungs and I do not fail three consecutive financial saves in a row!

KAITLYN: Throw wide the doors of death, Utah. Tonight, the file of dread closes.

SPENCER: Once and for all!

Chapter 15

Save Versus Advertisement

LM: *We are never, ever, ever–*

KAITLYN: It's the twelfth rendition, and I am still enamored with her, in both worlds.

UTAH: Right? Who is this incredible enchantress of realism? My flute is yours, m'Lady! Library Master, if you will tell us please.

LM: My friends, the singer is not here. Her voice is recorded in the boxes known as speakers, like as you heard in the Tiki Mermaid. Nevertheless, her message of dance and tranquility knows no physical, spiritual, or mental bounds. It is ephemeral. She is known as Tay, bringer of the swift lore. She of the festooned ornaments being shaken off. She of the bad

blood, and the wild dreams. But behold, are your eyes ready? Before you is quite the scene to see, as well as hear.

UTAH: On behalf of the Tiki's Mermaid, I stand ready to give my character's social reputation!

SPENCER: To default on his loans!

KAITLYN: To lose her sanity and if necessary, license to practice law!

LM: Your characters' courage has been noted. And now, for the part I've been wanting to read forever: You are now standing in a great gilded chamber, the likes of which appear royal, even for humans. A great circle of ornately carved columns holds up an impressive domed ceiling. Starlight and moonlight enter from the dome and mix in a cascade upon everything below. All around you plants and trees of every type grow in gigantic pots, they in turn are laced by the silver of the light. In the very center of the chamber stands an enormous marble statue of a man, and a woman, each holding a creature of the forest. The man wears a noble's attire, as befitting someone of stature and prestige in the real world. His face is adorned with a magnificent moustache which curls upwards like boars' tusks. Above his head, he wears a crown…er…no, that is not right. It is a hat, and this particular variety is a *cowboy's hat*-which if you'll refer to page 89 of your Man Manual contrasts with the rest of his attire. Yet somehow, the hat and the suit are attuned. He smiles amiably down at you as if to let you know that you are safe with him. Cradled in his arms is a raccoon, who lies on his back, legs outstretched in a playful manner. Clearly this friend of the forest trusts this man, inherently. At least in stone.

KAITLYN: What about the other one?

LM: Ah yes. The woman to his right sprouts a magnificent mane of flowing headhair, which falls over her well-endowed bosom. She wears a flowing dress, which even in rock, appears to be made of growing flowers and leaves unfurling along the curves of her torso and legs. Her eyes seem to twinkle with genuine sincerity, and her mouth is spread in a wide, happy grin. Lit on one outstretched arm is a magnificent eagle, wings at rest. The raptor's eyes are trained on the kind woman, as if awaiting a command from her mistress.

LM: Directly below the statue is a table, whereupon a goodly sized model of some new structure sits. Next to this model, sitting in a gilded chair, is the very real Matilda, owner and proprietor of the Tiki Mermaid. Matilda is holding a gilded pen, which hangs suspended in the air just above something flat lying on the table. You cannot see it well. She sips from a glass of water on the table, then sets it back down. Her face seems resigned to something. Above her is a magnificent watch, like the one that Selena showed you earlier, only much bigger. A short rod points to a number nine. A long rod points to a number twelve.

There is a shrill chime now from the watch. Matilda reaches out with her free hand and begins to open whatever is lying on the table.

UTAH: Noooooooooo!!!!!!!!!!!!!!!!!!!!!!!!!!!!!!

SPENCER: Matilda, STOP!!!!!!!!!!!!!!

KAITLYN: Library Master, I will enact my daily 2nd level immediate legal reaction, *chained chastisement*. Also, please note my familiar's innate power with flat objects of an inorganic nature.

LM: Please describe this in detail.

KAITLYN: The air crackles with my *legal authority*, as I loosen a bolt of *legalese* in all directions! "By the power vested in me by the legality of our human judicial institutions, I command thee to stop goodly barmaiden!" In the same instant, Meyers leaps from my back, somersaults in the air like a river otter in a waterfall, and lands upon what I assume can only be the very file we seek. He then slumps over to lay on his side, completely covering the file with his entire feline body.

LM: I'll allow it, but let's not get too carried away on the river otter thing.

UTAH: Meyer's body has closed the file?

LM: Yes. Before it opened.

SPENCER: How many pee yams are there?

LM: Nine.

SPENCER: And men-its?

LM: One.

UTAH: Then, the hour has expired. We've done it! Kaitlyn, you've done it! Meyers, you old clever cat-o-the-wild, bravo!

KAITLYN: But why do I feel like…

SPENCER: It was far too easy?

LM: A female voice as sweet as honey from the comb drifts into the chamber now. It is mixed with the lamentable lyrics of Tay, the swift lorist. You feel a type of insatiable need to listen to logic, real, inarguable logic. "Welcome goodly heroes of legal ethics," says the voice.

LM: And then, there is another voice, a male's voice. It is kingly, yet not imposing, "You have indeed closed the file, my nature loving friends! Your heroism is deserving of recognition. We welcome you and applaud your courage tonight. But behold, your barmaiden has already signed her tavern to our enterprise."

UTAH: It isn't so!

KAITLYN: I cast *finger of fine print* at Matilda. "Matilda, did you sign those papers?" This allows me to–

LM: Yes, I know. And there is no need to wonder. Matilda's face, flushed with a happy smile, is nodding up and down.

KAITLYN: To the music, or to my question?

LM: Both. The file may not have opened, but Matilda has signed over the Tiki Mermaid.

KAITLYN: Show yourselves you foul tavern stealing–

LM: Utah, your words are interrupted by two figures emerging from behind columns at either side of the statue. Each figure is identical in flesh to their carved likeness in stone, save that neither possesses their animal familiar. The larger of the two, the male Minick chuckles nonchalantly, "Now hold on just a minute, darlin', we didn't steal anything from your friend. Tell 'em Brittney."

LM: "That sure is right Benjamin," says the female Minick, "But don't take our word for it. Ain't that so, partner Matilda?"

LM: "Yes, yes that is so," says Matilda. She smiles and points to the model that lies on the table before you. Upon closer inspection, it is clearly more than a model of a human-made structure. You can see a small-scale version of the entire hillside adjacent to

the bay, where the Tiki Mermaid is built. However, in this model where the Tiki Mermaid once stood, now lies a much larger structure, with strange angles and shapes that seem to emulate a natural feature by some clever and logical design.

UTAH: I don't understand, Matilda. Why are you–

LM: "Allow me to explain ya' a bit amigos," says Benjamin. The man tips his hat, then he smiles and points to one of the small creeks in the model that flows around the Tiki Mermaid into San Deego Bay. "Ya' see fellers, we discovered through very careful scientific *anal sees* that the magnificent establishment known as the Tiki Mermaid's days were numbered."

LM: Brittney comes to stand by Benjamin's side. She leans up to kiss him on his cheek. Then looks at you all sweetly, "It's nature you see friends, nature has decided to play a cruel trick on Matilda's property. That is, until we decided to save it, *together*." She reaches out a bejeweled hand to Matilda, who takes it in hers. "And now, we simply aren't going to let that happen, are we honey bear?"

LM: Benjamin adds, "I know you saw the other models in our entryway, folks. Heck, that's why we left the doors open for y'all tonight. We wanted you to see our past mistakes."

SPENCER: Your mistakes?

LM: "That's right my bearded brother. We ain't proud of some of the past projects we've done. But now…"

LM: Brittney extends her other hand and squeezes Benjamin's, forming a smiling trinity between Matilda, Britney and Benjamin. "What my hubby means is…but now, we're going to make up for past wrongs, ain't we team? Hey, you see this statue? It shows our new commitment to the many natural spaces we haven't built anything on yet. You see how much that rascal there loves Benjamin." She points to the stone raccoon in the in the stone arms of Benjamin. "Gosh, it was fun rescuing him, wasn't it sweetums?"

LM: "It sure was," he responds. "Now listen, I imagine you folks didn't come all the way down here tonight, just to hear us lament about life before our metamorphosis. Y'all mind if we give you a bit of a pitch about this here project?"

SPENCER: Well…

LM: "Let's start with you Utah. You mind if I call you Utah? Say, great name by the way, bet you didn't even get that from a name generator or nothin'."

UTAH: Actually, I–

LM: "No matter. Say Utah, lookee here. See these little blue lines around the Tiki Mermaid? These are all just part of the local watershed, which sadly, is about to wash away the Tiki Mermaid, and destroy the habitat for many plants and animals in San Deego Bay. Now, you know that after we had our conversion, saw the light as it were, that we couldn't let that happen. So that's when we began to work on this here project, which is going to both save the Tiki Mermaid, and the bay's many creatures. Hey Utah, I heard you was a surfer, that so?"

UTAH: Well, yeah, I'm now a level–

LM: "Heck, then I bet you sure care about sea animals like seals and bat rays, right?"

UTAH: Yeah…

LM: "Well Sir, then you'll be glad to envision with me our Spicolli Animal Rescue Center, located right here."** Benjamin points to a part of the model lying over the bay on what appears to be wooden stilts, "This is going to be where we take care of 'em whenever one gets hurt. Say, you hungry Utah, I completely forgot that we had picked up some breakfast *burr ritos* earlier. We got an extra one right here, in fact."

UTAH: Well, yeah, of course, I'll take a breakfast bur rito. I mean, I didn't realize that the project was going to create a rescue center named after my–

SPENCER: Hold my horse's tail. Just how did you all transform yourselves, and what about the demons?

LM: "Everyone has demons, McAdams," says Brittney, still holding hands with Benjamin and Matilda, "McAdams, you're a fan of organic produce, am I right?"

SPENCER: Well, yes, but–

LM: "You see, based on human calculations over a lengthy, and I might add costly, span of time, when the Tiki goes, so too will the surrounding complexes of human dwellings known as *apartments*. These were constructed in the past with foul materials, that will break apart, polluting the bay with their loathsome essence. But thanks to our new design here, we've created a space right next to the bay where humans all throughout the city can come to buy locally sourced, organic produce at a truly one-of-a-kind farmer's market."

SPENCER: Locally sourced? Organic?

LM: Brittney chuckles a bit. "Hey, I know it's all hard to believe. But that's what good design does. It just makes everything better, without harming a soul. Hey McAdams, aren't you a fan of micro-brews?"

SPENCER: Am I!

LM: "Well then you'll be glad to know that the Spencer McAdams Farmer's Market and MicroBrew Plaza allows only all-natural ingredients, and the landscaping we've designed contains only native plants which will draw endangered butterflies and hummingbirds."

LM: Brittney takes over, "We've already got a dozen micro-brewery partners on board McAdams." She snaps her fingers. "You know what? You should try some of them-right now! Here," Brittney steps away for a moment, and when she returns, holds two pints of frothy golden ale out to you.

SPENCER: Locally sourced? All organic?

LM: "Of course," says Brittney smiling.

LM: "You know what my man," says Benjamin. "Why don't you just take a minute and think about everything. We'll answer any questions you have, after all," he tips his hat to Matilda, "We know we've got some trust to earn back since our transformation."

SPENCER: Well, I would love a couple of –

LM: "Oh hey, why don't you let me just take that jacket from you, McAdams. Then, you can sit here and enjoy–"

SPENCER: Oh, I can't take it off. It's cursed."

LM: "I see," says Brittney. "I've heard about such a condition. But you are listening to the swift lorist."

SPENCER: She's great.

LM: "Of course, she is. And did you know that while within her enchanted voice, curses, depressions, and pessimisms are ineffective? Seriously, give it a try. That is, if you'd like to.

SPENCER: I'd like to try and take off the jacket of narcissism!

LM: You remove one arm easily, then the other as well. The jacket slides off your shoulders as easily as a frog sliding off a lilypad. Benjamin and Brittney glance at one another, and smile at you. Brittney extends her hand towards you Spencer. "That's it, McAdams, almost there. Now just hand the jacket ov–"

KAITLYN: Wait. Something feels…

LM: Benjamin says, "Ah, you're the infamous Kaitlyn Jacoby we've been hearing so much about. And this must be your lovely familiar Meyers laying on the desk. Kaitlyn, we've been looking forward to meeting you most of all."

KAITLYN: Why?

LM: "Well, because," says Benjamin, "since our transformation, we've come to a realization. We need a partner at the law firm."

LM: Brittney, still reaching for Spencer's jacket, says, "Honey bear, how'd you like to quest over the land of San Deego, and beyond to unknown realms.

Wherever you go, you can use your powers of legalese to help the goodly folk, to save nature's animals, to essentially spread happiness everywhere you go?"

KAITLYN: Like pixie dust?

LM: "Yeah, that's right," says Brittney, fingers searching for the jacket. "Like pixie dust."

LM: "All you need," says Benjamin, now reaching towards the jacket too, "Is just to let us have this here jacket and to just give us this jac–

KAITLYN: Wait! Wait! This isn't right. Library master, I will save versus advertisement!

Chapter 16

Save Versus Snackage

LM: Your save was successful.

KAITLYN: Yes!

LM: And now you will, you all will, roll for initiative.

SPENCER, UTAH: Snapping turtle!

UTAH: But why would we want to enter debate with these fine–

KAITLYN: Reveal your true selves! I abolish the persuasive techniques of authority you have perpetrated on us. I command you fiends of finance! Debt deceivers! You... devel-lopers!

LM: Utah. Thanks to Kaitlyn's save, you've just escaped with your very financial lives. Upon her legal command, the devel-lopers *charismatic spray* is banished-their grand illusion of rhetoric is gone. Before you, the figures of Minick and Minick transform back into their true *developing* selves. All traces of their aggrandizing advertisement are washed away.

SPENCER: Their true selves are kind and generous?

KAITLYN: No McAdams! They are not kind and generous! They are vile and dreadful.

LM: You now see that Benjamin's suit does not attune to his cowboy hat in the slightest. In fact, the suit exhibits an aura of power over others, while the hat has a dweomer of doing what humans call *dirty work*.

SPENCER: What we call fun?

LM: Exactly. The hat is his way of bonding with those who do not have as much treasure in their chests. Moreover, his resting face wrinkles do not align with the smile he has been showing you. Illusion gone, he makes his typical human facial expression conforming to these wrinkles, which is one of disgust and arrogance.

UTAH: Oh my gods.

LM: Yeah. And worse is Brittney. Because her change is a little like watching a candle's wax melting. Her face, frozen to that point in a wide grin, now falls into a dramatic frown of elitist disappointment in *you*. You see now that her hair is colored with unnatural chemicals, not because of her time frolicking in the sun amongst nature. Her hand, still reaching for the jacket, is splotched, covered by a vast amount of toxic ointment. She has attempted to cover her true colors.

SPENCER: I put the jacket back on!

UTAH, KAITLYN: You what?

LM: Brittney is now screeching with a type of insecure rage known as *elitist fragility*. It's not an action. Just part of every Lah Hoyan's background. She gasps, "Give me the blazing jacket you fool! I've had enough of your second-class doings tonight! Lazlo, come out and help me fix what you have gone out of your way to ruin, you rapping idiot! Benjamin, do something here!"

LM: Benjamin puts his fingers in his mouth and makes a whistling noise like a shrill songbird, "Bandit! SkyMaster! Mama needs us!" In but an instant, the entire scene has morphed into a nightmare.

SPENCER: The four legged variety or…?

LM: No, the other kind.

UTAH: Oh thank goodness.

LM: Well not so fast! From behind the potted trees and shrubs, three shadowy shapes appear. Stepping into the light, you see none other than the dea jay, Lazlo, and his two henchmen. "Well, well, lookey who we got here," whistles Lazlo. "It's the super poser trying to represent 'rond town, ma homies. Sup loser. You ready to give me that jacket after I kick yo' ass"

SPENCER: No one kicks my ass, or any other beast of burden!

LM: Despite Kaitlyn's save, as you can now tell, you've all been surprised. Even Matilda seems to be watching the events unfold in a type of trance.

KAITLYN: Financially charmed.

LM: Not telling. But lo! There is a hissing chitter from behind the devel-lopers. And in a flash, a striped black and white furrball whizzes through the air. It's pointy whiskered nose, and four outstretched little claws seek Spencer's face. "Seek Bandit," shouts Benjamin, "Bring yo' daddy his jacket now you varmint!" You see it all in slow motion, the rabid raccoon arcing over the scene towards the hipster. Behind it, there is an echoing screech, and you see a blurred set of magnificent wings flapping. It is a golden eagle. It too has its talons outstretched before

it, aimed for McAdams as well. "Seek SkyMaster!" screams Brittney, her eyes closed with self-righteous indignation. "Bring Mama what she needs!"

SPENCER: I thought these gentle forest creatures were friends of goodly folk!

LM: Your foes all close in on you now. Benjamin howls with delight, "Ha! We found these two in abandoned nests during one of our many land clearings. We were going to let the graders cover them up like we do with the other pests-but then we had an idea. We figured that they would give us just the *environmental capitol* we'd need to fool stupid tree hugging types like you into signing your lives away."

LM: "And we were right," adds Brittney, whose eye paint is now running down her cheeks. Her now wraithlike eyes glimmer red in their sockets, "You're always the same. Every single project we do. All we have to do is throw you a little something that makes you feel better, and the development is a go! This time would have been exactly the same had it not been for Lazlo's idiocy leaving the note in his jacket pocket. Could have ruined the whole venture." Spencer, you are now being clawed at by Bandit, and SkyMaster is flapping his wings all around you. The bird's talons grip the dea jay's jacket, pulling it over your head.

LM: Benjamin pushes a button on the top of the table, and by some logical method, the entire model

flips over, only to reveal a second model which had been hidden below the table. This model features nothing like what the devel-lopers had shared with you earlier. It shows San Deego bay with buildings all around it, mahls, and of course, a gleaming San Deego Bay temple to the demon Mack Donald! It is clutches of turtle eggs times larger than what you had first seen. There is no rescue center, no farmer's market, and no area for aquatic animals to rest after a day of splashing and enjoying themselves. All is finally revealed.

SPENCER: I may need some pixie du—

LM: Let's debrief a bit. The file has already opened. And you are surrounded by the enemy. "McAdams," says Benjamin calmly, "Our surprise round is now at an end. As you can see, you are overwhelmed and overmatched. Give us the jacket, sign a *non-disc losher form*, and we will give you a low-paying job working in one of the water-front hotels without any medical insurance or time-off. If you do not, we will be forced to issue a *cease and desist*, and sue you for trespassing, which carries a penalty of one hundred dollars!

SPENCER: But that would total party bill us!

UTAH: What did we expect, it's the BBEGs!

LM: I will give you all a moment to consider the deal. But I warn you not to underestimate the power of these two fully laired devel-lopers, or their well-laid

plot. McAdams, you will be at the top of the order when you're done deciding.

UTAH, KAITLYN, SPENCER: (Unintelligible)

LM: Um, mind if I ask what you...

UTAH, KAITLYN, SPENCER: (Unintelligble)

LM: I see. You three think you are going to metagame this. Well McAdams, it's your turn.

SPENCER: I would like to use my action to give the jacket to SkyMaster.

LM: Remember friends, nobody ever really survives this part of the adventure. You can play File of Dread ten times and still not–

SPENCER: And I will then tell Lazlo that I saw his mother kicking a small broken box down the street the other day.

LM: Anything else?

SPENCER: Yep. And I tell him that I asked his mother what she was doing, and she said, "Lazlo and I are moving our unhappy home to a new place in the forest where there are no friends nor fireflies nor twilight parties." And since I gave the jacket to the eagle, I just want to be sure the LM knows that my two arms are stretched upwards.

LM: Well, yes.

UTAH: And now it is my turn, is it not? I realize I am currently holding the breakfast burr rito, so I will save versus snackage. And I make it! I toss the burr rito in the air to McAdam's outstretched arms, and with my quick action I place both myself and the male Minick inside of the hill giant's hula.

LM: Based on your rolls you succeed. But I honestly have no idea what you lot think you are–

UTAH: Yes!

KAITLYN: Meyers and I are next of course.

LM: "And I suppose you too are going to make us destroy your financial future!" Oh, that's a devel-loper talking. Not me.

KAITLYN: Not quite, nature-hater! I point two fingers, er, I mean, one finger at a window. "Look," I say, "there's an area with no lights down by the cove that some sneaky devel-loper could probably build some *condos* on." I then (unintelligible).

LM: Well, well, well, fellow forest creatures. I see you refuse to go down unless you go all the way down. Your attempt to use logic must be sung about sometime. But I fear you've forgotten just exactly what manner of humans you are up against. First, Lazlo, counters your roast with a comeback of his own. "That's the sorriest roast I've ever heard, poser. Besides, I just saw yo' mama this morning. She was returning a donut because it had a hole in it."

SPENCER: Did it though?

LM: Doesn't matter. Lazlo's won this round.

SPENCER: But his mama–

LM: No. You rolled a one Spencer, I am sorry.

SPENCER: Worth a try.

LM: The devel-lopers now take their turns. Benjamin, momentarily immobile inside of the hoop, instead uses a lair action, a once daily. Centering a zone upon himself, he creates an *air of pessimism*. All decisions not involving the use of his financial help will fail if you do save, at disadvantage.

UTAH: Ouch.

LM: And now the other Minick takes her turn. She activates her *gaze of self-righteousness*, which grants her a +3 and any opponents a -3 to all social attacks made against her. She then snatches the jacket out of the air with one hand from SkyMaster, and with her other hand, pulls the file out from under Meyer's sprawling body. Head tilted back, she cackles like a witch at midnight, "It is over fools! We have the signed papers from Matilda! We have the note that Lazlo left in his jacket. It could have gotten us into some legal trouble for sure. But now, that is no matter. Surrender, and we will not call law enforcement over your trespass!"

LM: "MUA HA HA HA HA!!!!" Oh that's not me again, it's the Minicks.

SPENCER: I'm up. I say to Lazlo, "You're mama is so pretty that even the faeries accept her into the twilight meadow!" And with my human hands in the air, I'd like to wave their tips, the…fingers… around and catch the burr rito. Then I shall feed it to the rabid raccoon currently attacking my torso.

LM: Done.

SPENCER: Did he like it?

LM: Doesn't matter. He's a raccoon. He'd have to crit now to save versus snackage. Well done, sort of.

SPENCER: What do you mean?

LM: Remember those seven potions you imbibed?

SPENCER: Yeah.

LM: Their effects did stack. All of them. You have just fallen unconscious, overdosed on *caff fien*.

SPENCER: Oh deer. I'm sorry team, I thought I'd….*snore*.

LM: It's just you and Kaitlyn now, Utah. Are you sure you don't want to–

UTAH: Never! I will attempt to use *surfer's grace*. I'll drop into a balanced stance, then throw my surfboard onto the floor. With a little hop, I will attempt to jump on top of it, slide over, and snatch the jacket from Brittney, the other Minick.

LM: That's quite the set of actions Utah. And based on your roles I have good brew and bad brew.

UTAH: Bad brew.

LM: Your attempt succeeds, until just the precise moment you lunge for the jacket. Benjamin Minick activates his immediate reaction, and uses *despotic sacrifice* on one of Lazlo's henchmen. He lunges in front of Brittney, causing 3d6 points of head trauma to you both. I am sorry Utah, but you've used your head for the last time tonight. You too, are unconscious-a heap of humanity lying on the floor at your enemies' feet.

UTAH: I'm sorry Jacoby and Meyers. I'm sorry San Deego. I'm sorry Tiki Mermaid.

LM: And then there was one. Kaitlyn Jacoby. You are now surrounded by Lazlo and a henchman, two greater devel-lopers, one of whom holds the two parts of your doom in each of her hands. You are the last of your party standing in their lair. Do not make them destroy your emotional intelligence.

KAITLYN: No, no. I don't want any of that. I put my hands up in the air, like I read about in page 145 of the Man Manual when humans surrender. "Well, you got us," I declare. "I don't suppose that offer to join your law firm still applies?"

LM: "No," hisses Brittney.

KAITLYN: I didn't think so. Well, I will leave now, and let you all have your way with the city. I don't suppose I can take a minor action and at least attempt to uncharm Matilda. It would be nice to leave the adventure with some dignity after this pitiful final battle.

LM: I'll allow that. Er…I mean the devel-lopers allow it. Brittney whispers some legal jargon in Matilda's ear, ending her financial charm. Matilda is distraught-her eyes flooding with tears.

KAITLYN: I reach out my hand to carefully pick up Meyers and place him inside of my backpack. I reach my other hand out to take Matilda by the hand. Then, I turn to leave, but pause. "There's just one thing though," I say to the Minicks, turning back around.

LM: "Oh, what's that darlin'?" snaps Benjamin triumphantly.

KAITLYN: Well, you see. I think you folks forgot how nature tends to work.

LM: "Oh enlighten us, honey," says Brittney. "We've used nature to enrich ourselves for–"

KAITLYN: "Oh I know it," I say. "And that's why I'm so surprised that you don't understand it better. Take cats for example. Anyone in the wild knows that when a feline lays down, nothing underneath it gets snatched away, but what it wants to be snatched away.

LM: "Well, that's nice," answers Brittney, "But I've already pulled the file out from under Meyers, and have it right here in my hand."

KAITLYN: Oh, you got the file alright. But what about what was in it?

LM: "You're bluffing," say both Minicks at the same time. Matilda stares at you.

KAITLYN: And what about your precious letter that you claim Lazlo kept in his jacket?

LM: What about it? This is me now, not the Minicks. You all observed it and Spencer put it back into his jacket pocket again.

KAITLYN: Did he? I was the one who last read the letter just before we entered Bart's market!

LM: Well, I–

KAITLYN: Behold! I remove both the letter from Spencer's jacket as well as the signed paper from Matilda that had been in the file. Meyer's, on my command, kept it hidden under his hairy belly, allowing the female Minick to remove the file from around it only! I also rolled a nineteen to secretly snatch it away from under Meyers when I picked him up, and I of course had kept the letter for myself all along. Ask any of us, I never gave it back to the hipster.

UTAH: Snapping turtle!

SPENCER: She's right!

LM: Quiet! You both are emotionally and financially dead, remember! Besides, this is all resolvable. Brittney snaps her fingers, "Lazlo! Bring me those damned documents on the double!"

KAITLYN: Oh, and I know it's Lazlo's turn here, so I know I am a goner and everything, but before he takes the papers, may I just ask one thing?

LM: One. Single. Thing.

KAITLYN: You forgot to tell us who won the final round of the yo' mama joke battle, before Spencer went unconscious.

LM: Well, that's because it didn't matter, you see I–

KAITLYN: Doesn't it? Hmm. According to page 156 of the Law Firms and Librarians Player's Manual, a human engaged in a roast with another human must receive a roast back in order to fail the roast attempt.

LM: So?

KAITLYN: So…that means Spencer saved versus yo' mama!

LM: So what?

KAITLYN: Well, according to page 87 of the Man Manual, anyone who had recently worn rapper attire *of any kind*, and who is the victor of a roast, imparts, *automatically*, the rewards of the roast onto all other members of the party.

LM: So?

KAITLYN: So, I turn to Lazlo, and ask him, "Who's yo' mama now?"

LM: This is rules-lawyering!

SPENCER, UTAH: But she's a lawyer!

KAITLYN: Please goodly Library Master, would you mind telling us all, what he says in response?

LEVEL 3

Chapter 17

Quest for the Smart Foan

UTAH: So, what did Lazlo say to Kaitlyn?

LM: Well, it wasn't much. Lazlo was still reeling from McAdams' roast. Apparently, humans only say pessimistic things during a yo' mama battle. But remember that the Minicks had created an air of pessimism.

UTAH: Right. So?
LM: So, a little known fact about it is that anything that is optimistic, actually has advantage.

SPENCER: So, I won the roast by doing the opposite of what humans normally do? By being my fae-self?

LM: You sure did.

SPENCER: Wow.

UTAH: And so then what happened? I was…er…unconscious, remember?

KAITLYN: Haha. Right. Sometimes a pixie has to do all the work herself around the swamp.

LM: Indeed. In summary *Spicolli*, Lazlo decided that Kaitlyn had something he referred to as *phunk*. He and his henchman woke up their unconscious brethren, kept the devel-lopers at bay, and guarded your flank as you exited the lair. Once outside the castle, I mean building, Selena drove you all back to Bart's bus. Matilda opened a different file which contained something called *law suits*. Wearing these law suits, she and Kaitlyn then battled the devel-lopers in something called a court, and guess what?

UTAH, SPENCER: What?

LM: They won! Of course, you didn't know any of that because you slept for about 3 days.

KAITLYN: Why three?

LM: Well, let's just say that you slept one for every level you have now acquired.

KAITLYN, SPENCER, UTAH: Woot!!!!!

LM: And now my friends, it is time to read you the last of the prepared descriptions. I confess, I did not think we would get there.

UTAH: Well, let's have it then. How does our adventure end?

LM: Hmmm mmm…On a night scented with the sweet smell of torch aloe and salted with ocean mist, you've all returned to the Tiki Mermaid-*still* the proudest ale house in all of San Deego.

KAITLYN, UTAH, SPENCER: *Still.*

LM: Friends, it has been a fortnight since your heroic victory in Lah Hoyah. Since then, you've enjoyed the city, the human people, and especially the incredible human food. At some point, Matilda needed help with new quests and hired you. Some were dangerous, but you survived.

SPENCER: What foul creatures did we battle this time?

LM: No beasts. But you were placed in charge of something known as a *deep friar*. The friar was nowhere to be found, but you did learn how to drop human food of every conceivable shape and size into a vat of boiling acid. Then, when the food was pulled out you coated it in salt and drenched it in a rain shower of something called *catch-up*.

UTAH: Did we like it? Any effects? Did the friar die in the acid?

LM: Um, yes and yes and most likely yes. Humans call the logical process that happens in the acid *kemus-tree* and when the food emerges it has a flavor as if it came from the astral plane. You've each gained 15 pounds of fat reserves—

KAITLYN: Sweet nectar, what a gift!

LM: But your speed modifiers have each been reduced by half.

SPENCER: Worth it.

LM: You've earned some good folding money from performing this quest. And no, nobody fell into the acid where presumably the friar's death somehow enchants the food now. I rolled. After that, Bart needed your help with a few things as well. Did you assist him?

SPENCER: Of course, we did. I love this quest narration stuff by the way.

KAITLYN: So...what did we find out?

LM: Well, first Bart asked you to keep a record of every time one of those air mounts called planes flew overhead. Then, you were to do something called *jernaling*. Bart asked you to talk to yourself in runes about the smoke the creature left in the sky behind it.

UTAH: That's jernaling?

KAITLYN: It's something humans do to keep track of their feelings.

SPENCER: Why would they do that? Who needs to keep track of a feeling? Just go frolic in the meadow and get it all out.

KAITLYN: Ask the will-o-wisps for a light show. Always cheers me right up.

UTAH: Right?

LM: Whatever the reason, you get the human instinctual feeling that Bart is taking this jernaling very, very seriously. You will be glad to know that he is paying you in items from his shop.

SPENCER: Snapping turtle! I'm going to stock up on turds.

UTAH: Me too!

LM: He also lets each of you take a turn from a sort of magical spout under an enchanted box of some kind. He shows you how to push a button, and when doing so an endless sweet nectar is loosed from the spout, directly into your mouth. Want the taste of strawberries in springtime? Push the red button. Want the flavor of blueberries ripe on the tree, press blue. You've never experienced anything like it.

UTAH: I'd like to stick my face under it until it stops giving me nectar, or I pass out.

LM: You pass out.

SPENCER: Amazing.

LM: Indeed. Bart calls it a *slurp pey*. He invites you to slurp from the enchanted spout anytime you'd like. He only asks that you don't do it while other customers patronize the store and that you quit before you pass out.

KAITLYN: A gift from the gods.

LM: Spicolli, you have caught many waves and surfed on all of San Deego's famous beaches. But it gets better. Selena has even taken you to 1d6 secret surf spots which has—

UTAH: Six!

SPENCER: Dude!

LM: Which has given you…600 logic points towards level 4! As you know a surfer's ability to tap into *stokage* from multiple surf spots enhances nearly all of his powers considerably.

UTAH: Have I kissed her again?

LM: Oh yes. Countless times. But benefits from these kisses do not stack unfortunately.

UTAH: Worth a try.

LM: McAdams, you've traveled far and wide among the hipster hamlets of San Deego. Hill Crest and South Park. Quest after quest, you have left no ale behind. You've tasted many fine beers, and as a result, your influence in the beer culture has become something of legend. In fact, one of your most popular ales is now toasted in your honor.

UTAH: Oh! Can we name it?

LM: Sure. McAdams, what do you call your famous ale?

SPENCER: I call it…I call it…

KAITLYN: Human Drink?

UTAH: Unicorn Piss?

SPENCER: Those are pretty good…but no…

KAITLYN: The Beer of Human Heroes?

UTAH: Better Than a Kiss Beer?

SPENCER: I call it Critical Ale!

UTAH: I like that.

LM: Not bad McAdams. Let's turn our attention to Jacoby here. Kaitlyn, you have provided the Tiki Mermaid with the unprecedented legal partnership to establish conservationist practices that are

reproduced and supported by countless businesses in the downtown area.

KAITLYN: Listen to you use all that rhetoric!

LM: Perhaps as a thank you, one day Matilda decides to add several figures to her mermaid mural behind the bar. She paints in a narwhal swimming above her already infamous mermaid. It's magnificent horn just breaks the ocean surface. She paints a faun riding a surfboard on a wave in the background, by Mission Beach.

SPENCER: Do you think she knows?

LM: But her masterstroke here is that she paints a second mermaid swimming beside her mermaid's likeness. This one has billowing blond hair too, trailing in the ocean current. The likeness to Kaitlyn is of course uncanny. And she spends a cornucopia of time working on it.

KAITLYN: I'd like to offer to help Matilda stock her shelves one afternoon.

LM: Do you want to help her with the ones in the closet? Or the ones right in the open?

KAITLYN: Oh, right in the open, please.

LM: Well done. And now here you all are, at the new and improved Tiki Mermaid. It looks better than ever thanks to the *lawsuit of extreme compensation*

that Kaitlyn created with her new level 3 legal abilities. With the folding money, Matilda completely expanded her bar's seating area. All around you cheers erupt as the fellow humans you've encountered in San Deego toast to the heroes who saved the Tiki Mermaid. With each toast there are three cheers for Utah Spicolli of the Surfboard! Three cheers for Kaitlyn Jacoby of the legal documents and her trusty assistant, Meyers. Three cheers for Spencer McAdams to whom the city owes thanks for his miraculously invigorating, Critical Ale. Selena is there with Utah and yes, you receive a kiss in this very moment which indeed does stack in large communal gatherings. In the corner, you see Lazlo consoling Deuce Brockit. He apparently lost his sponsors one day recently after he was found one afternoon to have used his wax of sexing in a public bathroom.

UTAH: Human rules are still so weird to me.

LM: But fear not, because Lazlo has work for him. Deuce will use the muscles he developed surfing to carry musical equipment for the dea jay at all of his events now.

SPENCER: Look at all our new human friends.

LM: And so, a typical human night unfolds around you all. Human people talk with one another, while the sounds of enchanted music from boxes fills the evening air. People smile with their lips and enjoy their beers by swallowing, and not slurping. The sun

is setting through the windows, and you are all the talk of the bar. And well, that's the end, everyone.

UTAH: Wait, what? Dude, you can't just end the adventure like that!

LM: Why not? It's a perfect stopping point.

SPENCER: Because…because we want to play these human characters again!

KAITLYN: Exactly.

LM: You do?

KAITLYN: Duh! That's Eng Lish for 'of course' by the way.

LM: But I thought this was going to be a one shot?

KAITLYN: Well, it was until you went and made all this awesome logical stuff happen and we saved the entire city and I can use jargon and Spencer invented Critical Ale.

SPENCER: Besides, this hipster class is really the faun's flute.

UTAH: You flatter me my hoofed friend.

SPENCER: You know what I mean, Spicolli.

LM: Are you sure you want to…okay, okay. Let me just see here…ah yes, it's in the appendices. Several

options to choose from looks like. But someone will need to give me a roll. A d4 ought to do it.

UTAH: Four.

LM: Oh, that's a really good one. But I'm not sure you all will—

KAITLYN: Come on then. What does it say?

UTAH: Out with it, bro.

SPENCER: You know you are really starting to sound like your char—

KAITLYN: Let's have it!

LM: Okay, okay. Look there is a problem apparently with an order for the bar. It's a very, very large order of...your beer--Critical Ale, actually.

SPENCER: My beer has a problem? Oh, this cannot stand!

LM: Well, you see Matilda began to cater to large events. Your friend, the conspiracy theorist Bart, needed a quest and so everything sort of fell into place like dew on flower petals. Bart uses his driving feat to transport beer to festival events even in different towns. It just so happens that an enormous supply of beer was loaded onto a caravan to a nearby town called...it's here somewhere, ah yes...Lost Magus. It's in the Merry Can desert. Very hot

climate. But apparently many humans still like to go there. And it says here they bring a lot of folding money and coin money with them.

KAITLYN: Finally, a town that makes a bit of sense, right?

SPENCER: So? A problem with my beer, go on.

LM: Well, as Bart is about done loading the brew, Matilda has lost her most precious logical item, her *foan*.

UTAH: I heard of those! Very, very logical.

LM: Yes, all humans acquire one at level 5.

SPENCER: Changes everything about the game is what a bugbear told me a few twilights ago.

KAITLYN: I've been drooling over one ever since I saw it in Humans and History! What kind is it? I heard there are many types.

LM: It's a very special type. Called a *smart* foan. Hers is quite powerful. It's a *smart foan of telepathic messages*-a plus 3. Apparently, it's so smart that it knows where the wheeled mount needs to take the loaded ale all by itself.

UTAH: Wow.

LM: Yeah, but she can't find it anywhere. And human mounts do not have brains or instincts like ours do in our world.

SPENCER: Where shall we start looking?

KAITLYN: Let's use logic. After all, we're practically people now, right?

UTAH: Totally. Okay, where was the last place that Matilda remembers having it? Oh, snapping turtle! I critted on my investigation.

LM: Nice Spicolli. For that, you know that the exact location she remembers being with her foan was in the back of the wheeled mount where the beer is loaded. It's just behind the Tiki Mermaid.

UTAH: Well, then that's where I'm headed.

SPENCER: Me too.

KAITLYN: Me three of course. And I'll bring Meyers with me just in case we need a creature with a decent ability to smell.

LM: Well, behind the Tiki Mermaid, the large, wheeled mount sits, and its back doors hang open on either side. Inside are piled massive barrels filled with Spencer's delicious Critical Ale.

UTAH: We climb inside and begin to search.

LM: All of you?

SPENCER: Sure. Never separate humans *in* a party.

KAITLYN: Duh.

LM: Well, I've got good brew, and bad brew. Which do you want first?

SPENCER: Let's go good brew first for once.

LM: Well, the good brew is yours. There is plenty of it in the belly of the mount.

KAITLYN: And the bad brew?

LM: Firstly, you do not find a foan. Secondly, just as you climb inside, the doors shut behind you! You hear a man, might be Bart, whistling to himself, and another door slam. Then, the entire beast roars angrily and sputters. You are in the belly of the beast, trapped, as it comes to life!

UTAH: I push on the door, pull on it, try to break it.

KAITLYN: I yell for Bart, for anyone! I use the *sror tee* sisters wail! Why won't he open it?

LM: You aren't sure. But he appears to be whistling a tune from the lorist, Tay.

UTAH: He's entranced. He couldn't hear a thing even if he wanted to!

SPENCER: Oh my swamp, this thing is going to consume all my beer, and then us! Why didn't we end this when we were ahead!

LM: I am sorry humans. But the door is impossible to open from the inside. You see, a clever logical human device has been activated on the outside. Also, Kaitlyn does not know how to wail like a *sror tee* sister, and Spencer is clearly in shock.

UTAH: I guess we will just have to wait to see where this foul beast takes us.

SPENCER: And how long it takes to be digested.

LM: I can only answer one of the questions tonight. Which do you want?

KAITLYN: Let's go with where it is taking us. I already know how long the digestion process will most likely take because Regofran the dwarf that one time told us about how these halflings were messing around with that behir and then he found their bones—

LM: Okay my friends. But this is truly it for tonight. You are all on your way to Lost Magus, a town very different than San Deego. A town that, should you survive the digestion process, should no doubt need your help, too.

UTAH: I tap one of the kegs and drink a human handful.

KAITLYN: Me too! Two hands!

SPENCER: Me three, and I'll use---oh wait, right, two hands!

UTAH: A toast to being digested! Marinated in our own ale!

KAITLYN: Hear, hear!

SPENCER: Smell, smell!

LM: The...end...

UTAH: But also...to be continued.

UTAH: Oh wait...before we go.

LM: Yes?

UTAH: We planned to meet at the next full moon, right?

LM: That's what I wrote on my scroll.

UTAH: Well, sorry team but I said I'd help Lenndrix the wizard with his acolyte training that day. Apparently, he has a group of adventurers that can't seem to understand how to engage with fae folk.

SPENCER: Actually, that works for me because I told Magrugan the Wise that I'd grant her wish to finally drink from the enchanted fountain up past the Emerald Woods where that treant went off-root.

KAITLYN: Oh, I love that place. I might fly in with a few of my friends if you don't—

UTAH: You have my flute, noble unicorn!

SPENCER: Sounds like a prance!

LM: Okay, so then we will skip a moon but continue where we left off from here. This is really it then friends. To use a human word, it's officially…

The End

UTAH: For now.

Epilogue

Dear Human,

I hope you enjoyed listening in on some good friends play the first of Law Firms & Librarians adventure modules-The File of Dread. We loved having you here with us and the fairy folk of the brackish swamp at the edge of the elvish wood.

Now that we've heard all about their magnificent quest, let's use our imaginations again and see what happens now that their game is over. That's it, peak through the pond reeds with me here. Can you see the ogre pawing at his sore legs? Can you hear him yawning his great throaty yawn? That is a final sign that the night's gaming has certainly come to an end.

Ah yes, there they are. Once more we can see them there in the swamp, their game pieces on the boulder in the center. The ogre is placing their miniature figures, as gingerly as his clawed talons can of course, back into his rucksack. Meanwhile the others are dancing and twirling themselves in the brackish water at their hooves, except

of course for the pixie who is flitting between them.
Clearly, they are exalted in their deeds as imaginary yet
real humans. The pixie is sprinkling her dust all about in
a magnificent display of multi-colored cheer. It's been a
great night of pretending to be logical in the real world
for them all.

The unicorn stretches his forelimbs, careful not to catch
his perfectly twizzled horn on a lily pad. He tells the
others he has to see a gnomish caravan about a double-
rainbow that fulfills a prophecy for a dwarven enclave in
the morning.

The pixie flaps her hummingbird wings and
nonchalantly throws the last of her dust over the ogre,
who feigns to swat it away with a wry grin.

The faun plays his lute to a melancholy tune now. He
stops and stares off into the dark woods, and when an
answering silver-tuned note rings out, he waves goodbye
and bounds off through the trees.

The ogre is the last to leave. He ties the rucksack to an
old ship's anchoring chain, which he found a while back
in a bay at low-tide. He now uses the chain as a belt and
the anchor as a toothpick. Finally, he grunts into the
night, which sounds to my own ears like something in
crude giant about players using name generators.

You must surely need some sleep yourself. Perhaps you
too need to see a caravan about a double rainbow and a

prophecy in the morning. If you do not, remember you can always imagine that you can.

Speaking of which, perhaps we will use our imaginations again sometime and meet here at the edge of the brackish swamp in the future to see what the ogre has *in store* for his friends. That is, when next they find some time from their busy, magical lives. I certainly hope that we do.

As for me, I too have some things to tackle when the sun first sets over the hills beyond the elvish wood. I'd better blink myself to my nest before the pixie's dust wears off.

Life can't always be an adventure in reality.

One must keep to their fantasies a little too.

Appendix A: L&L Adversaries

The land of San Deego is populated with financially fearsome, socially awkward, mentally unstable, and rhetorically radical denizens of day and night. As your characters journey on their quest, they may encounter any and all of the following fearsome humans.

Carron Crawler
Frequency: *Common*
No. Appearing: 1-4
Social Class: 2
Drama Rating: 1
Bankruptcy Save: 15
Percent Medical Insurance: *100%*
Percent in Lair: *80% (20% Rotary Meetings)*
Treasure Type: *affluent, middle-aged*
Special Abilities: *Park Camouflage, Legaleze, Social Connection, elitist glare*
Special Defenses: *Flurry of False Facts, Jargon*
Logic Resistance: *None*
Alignment: *Chaotic Ignorant*
Rhetorical Ability: *35%*
R.P. Value: 400

Carron crawlers lurk in urban environments where they wait to spring their sinister trap. Difficult to identify by dress, age, or hairstyle as they come in many forms. Nevertheless, carro crawlers can most easily be identified by a type of accented lisp in their Eng Lish

(DC 15, greater carron, see also *prima donna*, DC 22). When carron crawlers detect a zone of social or emotional strength, they attempt to surprise their victims by springing out from bushes, trees, or from behind parked karrs. The carron crawler has evolved to speak a type of Eng Lish known as legaleze, which sounds to the untrained human ear to be important. In reality, carron crawlers have a very weak defense, and can be defeated easily with strong and consistent logic-or by alerting authorities.

Carron crawlers are most commonly encountered wearing *workout attire* that helps them to blend into the parks, parking lots and suburban sidewalks in which they dwell. Each carron crawler has a social connection that is the base of their special abilities. This social connection could be a mayor on the same street block in which they live, a cousin who married a councilman, or a husband who "people know well."

When a carron crawler detects a zone of social and emotional competency, they will first use their *jargon*, and *legaleze* to frighten off the intruder from their territory. Should they come under attack themselves, they will use first their *flurry of false facts* or *alternative facts* (level 5 and higher) and if need be their *social connection*. Carron crawlers do not easily allow themselves to be overcome by an opponent. If they feel as though their social class may be in jeopardy, they will use *park camouflage* to slink back and disappear. Then, they will wait to spring their trap again.

Conspiracy Theorist
Frequency: *Uncommon*
No. Appearing: 1*
Social Class: 9
Drama Rating: 4
Bankruptcy Save: 1
Percent Medical Insurance: *Low*
Percent in Lair: *100%*
Treasure Type: *nil*
Special Abilities: *Convention Gathering, Selective Hearing*
Special Defenses: *Flurry of False Facts*
Logic Resistance: *100%, Special*
Alignment: *Neutral Ignorant*
Rhetorical Ability: *Rumor Proficiency, Blog Posting*
R.P. Value: 100

The conspiracy theorist is a bizarre human creature that dwells predominantly in basements but can be found throughout both urban and rural environments. Conspiracy theorists are often dressed in strange garments, which usually appear as stained t-shirts. These garments have significant meaning to the theorists and on a DC17 or higher can help identify what type of conspiracy the theorist spends his days trying to solve. Some conspiracy theorists have gained an ability to camouflage as store clerks, uncles, and other typical non-player humans. Nevertheless, if questioned, conspiracy theorists will begin to divulge 1d4+2 rumors, some of which will be true, and some of which will be false (LM's discretion).

Conspiracy theorists will often avoid conflict, unless they appear in large groups of more than 100 people. Alone, conspiracy theorists will *blog*, and spread rumors in an effort to avoid debate or physical altercations. The conspiracy theorists most potent defensive attack is *Flurry of False Facts*, which they will use immediately when threatened. Logic does not affect them, as they have natural immunity to any thing that makes logical sense.

Although typically harmless, player characters may wish to avoid situations where conspiracy theorists are found in large clusters, such as at *Flah Thurth Conventions*. Legend holds that a more powerful type of conspiracy theorist exists known simply as *G*. Members of G's secret cabal are rumored to believe in dark and cryptic theories involving a mysterious entity known only as *The Scrump*.

Dea Jay, Lesser

Frequency: *Rare*
No. Appearing: 1
Social Class: 3
Drama Rating: 7
Bankruptcy Save: 7
Percent Medical Insurance: *nil*
Percent in Lair: *80%*
Treasure Type: Funk
Special Abilities: *Playlisting, Party Aura, Select Songs*
Special Defenses: *Bling, frontin', Music Minions*
Logic Resistance: *None*
Alignment: *Chaotic Playful*
Rhetorical Ability: *Nil*
R.P. Value: 1,000

The dea jay is a subterranean being that thrives on the human need to celebrate in social gatherings. Dea jays wear extravagant garments which may or may not include masks, helmets, hats (especially Fedo Rahs), scarves, and thick puffy jackets. Of course, this always includes the dea jays favorite accessory, known as *bling*, which a dea jay is never without, as it is the source of much of his/her power.

Typically, dea jays are not interested in logical debate or emotional conflict of any kind. However, should their ability to play music to throngs of human people be threatened, they will defend themselves and their *party*, with intense and complete ferocity.

In debate, dea jays typically attempt to *select songs* which can call forth 2d6+DJ level worth of *music minions*. In some cases, selected songs can establish a powerful illusion, especially when the dea jay works in concert with other enemies. If a dea jay must engage personally in debate, he/she will typically *front*, while selecting songs that create a *party aura*. Dea jays are known to contain vast treasure stashes of bling (which they keep safe around their necks) depending on their dea jay status (see chart).

Devel-loper, Greater
Frequency: *Very Rare*
No. Appearing: 1-2
Social Class: 1
Drama Rating: 2
Bankruptcy Save: *Immune*
Percent Medical Insurance: *nil*
Percent in Lair: *15%, 85% social gathering*

Treasure Type: Old Money or Self-Made
Special Abilities: *zone of jargon, finger of agreement, charm buyer, elitist glare, Scrump's small hand of narcissistic rage, finger of nepotism, narcissism's call, cone of itsforthegoodofthecity, zone of itsgoingtobebuiltanyway, gaze of self-righteousness, charismatic spray x1/day*
Special Defenses: *protection from sound reasoning 30' radius, finance drain, small print word salad, sphere of lets-make-a-deal (immediate reaction)*
Logic Resistance: *75%*
Alignment: *Lawful Narcissistic*
Rhetorical Ability: *Advanced*
R.P. Value: 10,000

The devel-loper is a powerful, financially occurring class of L&L enemy. Whenever a community of humans develops a certain level of wealth, 1d4 devel-lopers may discover opportunity and inhabit the area, often initially as city councilmen or women. Lesser devel-lopers do exist, but are rarely encountered in debate as they often spend their youth on *yots*, at *boarding schools* or *abroad*.

To become a greater devel-loper, the human must become empowered in a variety of skills, traits, and tactics which can take a human lifetime to master. At lower levels, devel-lopers use *elitist comraderie* and master the skill of *mingling,* both at will, and develop skill in *mixology, gastrology,* and *French literature* or *mid-century modern architecture*. Similar to the powers of a karen crawler, devel-lopers however establish a lair, which is used to send out social webs using *affluent connections* and *upper-class nepotism*. At some point thereafter, devel-lopers will use their inherent powers, *dabbling of real estate,* and *investments of passive income,* to gain property in their surrounding area. This is when the devel-loper has grown to full strength. When confronting a devil-loper, the party will hope that he or she can be drawn from its lair, but this is nearly impossible. Devel-lopers rarely leave their source of power, as they tend to stare at the pictures and models of their victims which they place on white pedestals at the entrance of their offices.

A devel-loper has a host of attacks for what they call *interlopers* and will use any and all of them for their amusement. In debate, a devel-loper will activate a *zone of jargon*, and immediately attack with *rhetorical assualt* (DC17) followed by *rhetorical passive threat* (DC19). During the ensuing debate, devel-lopers use their lair actions to create multiple areas of effect, all of which stack bonuses on them, and penalties on their opponents. These areas stay in effect for one full hour or until the devel-loper is defeated and include: *cone of itsforthegoodofthecity, zone of itsgoingtobebuiltanyway, Minick's Contradictory Law,* and *finger of nepotism*. Devel-lopers will rarely engage in physical attacks, preferring to acquire henchmen by either *finger of nepotism* or *narcissism's call*.

Should the battle be going poorly for a devel-loper, they will then use *legaleze, lawyer-speak* and *foan-a-lawyer* to escape to their yot. Once there, they will take 1d4 years to renew their powers in a different lair, all the while seeking their revenge on those who have spoiled their plans to build "something the world has been waiting for."

Dobble Gangsters
Frequency: *Uncommon*
No. Appearing: 2-12
Social Class: 8
Emotional Rating: 7
Bankruptcy Quota: *5-20 dollars*
Percent Medical Insurance: *25%*
Percent in Lair: *nil*
Treasure Type: *Broke*
Special Abilities:*fake a reputation, special* (see below)*
Special Defenses: *clique blend*
Logic Resistance: *None*
Alignment: *Neutral Playful*
Rhetorical Ability: *Low*
R.P. Value: 100

Although the gangster is a well-known part of L&L lore, the dobble-gangster is often a misunderstood part of modern human society. Because humans typically follow trends or patterns. ike birds of a feather, humans will often flock together.

The dobble gangster is a byproduct of this intense internal desire to belong. Using his *mimic swag* ability, the dobble gangster will attempt to infiltrate small groups of humans. Depending on age, gender, and utility, dobble gangsters will then leverage their skills to gain valuable assets which they use to gain finance, reputation or *narcissistic supply*. Typically, a dobble gangster will attempt to isolate a member of the infiltrated group, then copy their style and mannerisms. Then they use their *fake a reputation* ability to establish themselves in their victim's original social status. If this sneak attack succeeds, the victim will be abandoned from the group for 1d3 days or until the dobble gangster rolls a critical miss on any swag challenge, whichever comes first. While the dobble gangster has assumed their victim's position within the social group, they may use all powers and abilities that their victim was once afforded up to level 9.

Surfers and bartenders are natural enemies of the dobble gangster and gain a +3 to *detect poser* whenever a dobble gangster stands adjacent or in front of a surfer or bartender class human.

Hoam Boys
Frequency: *Common*
No. Appearing: 2-20
Social Class: 8
Emotional Rating: 4
Bankruptcy Quota: 3 dollars
Percent Medical Insurance: *0%*
Percent in Lair: *5%*
Treasure Type: Nil
Special Abilities: *frontin', saggin', so gangsta'*
Special Defenses: *youandwhosarmy, gang signs, tattoos of intimidation*
Logic Resistance: *50%*
Alignment: *Neutral*
Rhetorical Ability: *Med*
R.P. Value: 150

One of the most impressive specimens found in human cities is the hoam boy. Although a single hoam boy could no more than scare rabbit from its hole, a group of hoam boys, known as a *gang*, can pose quite a challenge during debate.

Hoam boys flock together in an effort to secure territory for which they can parade within. They use logical runes, written from *cans of spraying*, that tell other groups of hoam boys where boundaries lie. Additionally, hoam boys spend much of their time outdoors *frontin'*, and *saggin'* but these displays are often only meant for other hoam boys in ritualistic yet harmless display. Hoam boys can cast powerful auras that cancel debate actions against them like logic, rhetoric, and sometimes even legaleze and jargon. They are primarily susceptible to groups where the number of humans are greater than that of their group, and in the event that their pants fall completely off their hips.

Sror Tee Sisters
Frequency: *Common*
No. Appearing: 1
Social Class: 3
Drama Rating: 7
Bankruptcy Save: *Immune*
Percent Medical Insurance: *nil*
Percent in Lair: *80%*
Treasure Type: *nil*
Special Abilities: *hoochy, valley-girl mall stance, soa-khal lisp, wail of ohmagawding, zone of humiliation,*
Special Defenses: ohnoyoudidint, cleavage blast, bubble-gum snap (immediate reaction)
Logic Resistance: *0%*
Alignment: *Chaotic Selfish*
Rhetorical Ability: *Nil*
R.P. Value: 300

Sror tees, commonly referred to as "sisters", are one of the most fearsome adversaries in all of Merrac Kah. Adventurers will find the most dreadful of these so-called sisters inhabit the coastal college hamlets right here in San Deego. Sisters are instantly recognizable by either their *hoochy* clothing, *bleached* blonde hair, or *valley-girl mall stance*. Sisters, like all humans, come in a variety of shapes and sizes, yet typically at least one of the before-mentioned traits will be enough to spot one or more of them.

Verbally, a sister may also be immediately identified whenever they speak on account of their *soa-khal lisp* (DC10). Like hoam boys, sisters are often harmless individually, and will speak *soa-khal lisp* or *dude* about a variety of topics which include but are not limited to: hair, clothing, other's hair, other's clothing, malls, *moovies*.

If encountering one sister, a skill check is needed (DC12) to discuss either South *Merry-kan* literature or poverty. However, should the party discover a cluster of sroar-tee sisters at either an event involving alcohol, at a shopping mall, or a festival involving dancing, they will have their two human hands full. The sisters will gather into a full ritualistic circle, whereupon they will raise their voices in unison and hunch towards one another, pointing or gesturing at random objects behind them. If one of their fingers points to a member of the party, the sisters will then create a *zone of jargon*, and cast *finger of humiliation*. If the finger of humiliation reduces any party member within the zone to become humiliated, they must exit the area until either they've purchased an item of exquisite craftsmanship, changed their hair's appearance in length or color, or after one full day, whichever comes first. Sror-tee sisters consume mostly carrot sticks, hummus and alcoholic beverages. A *zone of pizza* can create a sphere of safety from their most dangerous attack, *wail of ohmagawding* (DC14).

Appendix B: New Logical Items

The Board of Skay Ting

This piece of highly polished, sculpted wood appears to be a normal slab of large conifer hardwood. However, attached to the underside are spinning *wheels* that when placed on a downhill slope cause the entire device to move quickly over land, especially flat surfaces. Legend holds that a man, or woman, known as Skay Ting created the first board when he was being harassed by a foul carron crawler while trying to climb a park tree. He fell out of the tree, bringing the branch of wood he was holding onto with him. As fate would have it, he landed on some round decorative beach stones, rolled through a human *laundry line*, and all the way down a grassy knoll until he fell into San Dee Goh Bay. When he broke the surface, he not only had escaped his enemy but had also caught a fish for dinner, trapped in between the line and his board. Thus the board of Skay Ting and the use of human *fishing nets* were invented in the same day.

Board of *Sur Fing*

This piece of lightweight carved foam is shaped like a massive dragon's tooth, and is just as large. It is coated in a type of shiny glass which creates a logical resistance to water. Surfers are never far from their boards of surfing as these devices are used to catch waves of incredible sizes in coastal villages like sunny San Deego. A board of surfing creates a substance known as *stoke* or *stokage*. This mighty substance grants surfers their logical powers, physical, mental and social. A board of surfing is best ridden with *wax of sexing* (see Man Manual). Note that this wax differs in application from other products which humans use to make more humans.

Boogie Shield +1, +3 vs. children

The boogie shield is known only to the San Deego region. In its basic function it provides the user a +1 bonus to all attacks, excluding *ego taunts*. Ultra rare, this human invention can be used in as many ways as a player character can think to use it. With LM approval, the following chart can be used to find what function it will provide the bearer when properly held in either one or two of the human hands.

0-3   flotation device

30-50   shield +3 against attacks from sub-adolescent humans

50-6   serving platter

65-75   back-cushion or pillow

75-85   protection from lightweight and/or soft missiles

85-99   musical instrument (requires two hands be free of use)

00   fashion statement

Can of Effervescently Happy Snakes

Often found with other logical devices, a can of effervescently happy snakes mimics something magical due to its clever human design. Coiled lightweight pieces of metal covered in paper which mimic snake skin are placed into the can and the lid is then screwed on very tight. When the bearer of the can wishes to add humor to a burgeoning new friendship, they simply remove the lid quickly and the snakes fly out in all directions. Note that humans with different backgrounds may act differently to snakes than many creatures do in our world, therefore this item has a malfunction rate of 30%. If the LM rolls a 1-3 on a 1d10, the snakes will cause 1d4 humans in the nearby area to run screaming and cursing, rather than stay and share in a pleasant afternoon in the meadow.

Dea Jay's Jacket of Narcissism, Cursed

This magnificent yellow jacket has no equal. Its' design is unparalleled and is immediately noticed by any within a 40' radius. Dea jays wearing the jacket can summon 1d6 junior rappers at will, and gain a +4 to all performances with direct lighting. The jacket increases a dea jay's attraction modifier and all associated performance skills by +2, and boosts a dea jays ego by +3 while *frontin'*. Finally, a human of any class wearing the jacket of narcissism may conjure 2d4 yo' mama jokes at will which may be used to frighten away potential rivals on stage.

The jacket grants any dea jay wearing it incredible powers, but serves anyone who is not a performer class to become cursed and affected in all ways that are opposite to a dea jay's benefit. Only a successful yo' mama joke battle competition may allow the cursed victim to remove the jacket of narcissism. Therapists, bartenders, and crowbars are ineffective.

Hoop of Hill Giant Hula

This large ring of plassed tick is about as big around as a hill giant's nostril. When spun around the waist, arm, leg or neck, it creates an aura of *hula*. This hula is a mental attack (DC15) which causes a distraction for other humans up to a 30' radius. All those in the area of effect who bear witness to the spinning will be stunned for one round while they paint a mental picture of what they would look like in their minds doing the very same activity. The bearer may choose to extend the spinning for future rounds but with higher DCs. While spinning the hoop, the spinner can do nothing but shake their hips and sing fast-paced dance songs.

Spinning 1 round (DC 15)

Spinning 2 rounds (DC 17)

Spinning 3 rounds (DC 19)

Spinning more than 3 rounds requires at least one level in *circus-performer*.

Game of Dragons and Dungeons

Leave it to humans to invent so outrageous a creation. The Game of Dragons and Dungeons is packaged in a red box. The game directions are written on two scroll packets in bold type. Six gem-like stones are included as well as a stylus.

This game is still quite unknown in the magical world, but rumors do exist of humans using it to play creatures like themselves in our world. In some versions, they even play less humanoid-type beings, like ogres, pixies, fauns and even unicorns. The objective of the game seems to vary, but the basics can be summed up as follows. First, get together with some good friends. Second, tell a fabulous story of adventure using a mixture of fun and ingenuity. Sprinkle in some dragons (no idea why they substitute dragons here for pixie dust). And repeat whenever time permits.

The game, in essence, seems to be a rather creative version of Law Firms & Librarians, only set in our world, instead of that of the humans.

Goggles of Underwater Vision

These devices are placed over the eyes of humans typically while they swim underwater, thus granting them vision below the surface. However, when worn over the eyes on dry land, they create a cone in the field of human vision. All those potential breeding partners within that cone gain a +2 to their attraction modifier, and the wearer receives a -2 to their attraction modifier and a -4 to walking up and down stairs. The goggles have no other function.

Noodle of Poodling

A noodle of poodling is a device which is often found with a board of boogying. Much like its foamy partner, the noodle of poodling is used for a variety of purposes. To activate the noodle, one needs simply to use their human thumb and four fingers to create a circular ring around the noodle at either the top or bottom of the device. Then, it may be swung, stabbed, slapped or spoken through for a variety of purposes. Should a player character discover the noodle's secret activation word while in the presence of an adversary, the noodle may be used to playfight, create loud noises, or as a *gesture of embarrassment*. The secret activation word is *"on-guard."*

Turd of Oderiferous Emanations

Always found wrapped in plassed-tick, with detailed runes and a painted image about its use, the turd of oderiferous emanations is a powerful and potent defensive weapon. When this unassuming turd is removed from its packaging and thrust against a hard object, such as a floor, stone, or building, a strong aura of sickening odor pours forth. Well known in human lore, people are unable to even remotely smell or sniff objects that sicken them, cause them to vomit, or otherwise bring tears to their two eyes. Thus the turd of oderiferous emanations is often used to create a potent diversion, whereby an adventuring team can make their exit, or drive away opponents while in or before debate. It should be noted that the turd is best used in informal social situations. If the opponent(s) are professional, are at *an opera*, or otherwise have access to *law enforcement,* the effects of the turd will be the same, however, each member of the team will need to make a save versus bankruptcy and reduce their income by 5d8 +social situation modifier, (see chart).

A Vaca Dough

A vaca dough is most typically found in urban rester haunts, and is always accompanied by a portion of sliced bread or small triangles of pressed corn. This green slimy substance takes various consistencies but is most often found in appearance to that of pond mud. A vaca dough must be made by either a member of the Span Lish tribe, or a hipster to have maximum effect. When the vaca dough is prepared and placed visually before any human whose hunger quota is below 3, that human must roll versus *snackage* or immediately reach for the prepared morsel. The consuming victim may still take any and all actions, and their *purpose, ignorance and playfulness* modifiers are all unaffected. However, any of their two hands which hold the vaca dough will hinder their ability to do any and all physical tasks, and their distraction modifier will be doubled. Any debate skills will have disadvantage while a human is in the process of consuming the spread. Furthermore, if a human within twenty feet, who can both see and smell a vaca dough, has a hunger quota of 1, that human will be completely stunned for 2d4 rounds or until the entire vaca dough is consumed, whichever comes first.

Potion of Monster Energy

This potion grants the user 1d10 rounds of mental clarity and physical energy. During this period, any human consuming the potion will believe that their "world is wide open" and that finally they can "get something done." Once the potion wears off however, the imbiber will take no actions besides self-feeding and make passive comments only for 1 full hour. If more than three potions of monster energy are consumed at one time the period of mental clarity and physical energy will stack, as well as the potion's duration. However, when the effects wear off, the imbiber will completely urinate all over themselves, mumble incoherently and stare morbidly at anyone who moves within a 10' radius to where they sit motionless. Should a human imbibe more than three potions of monster energy five or more days in a row, the after-effects will become a permanently cursed condition and may only be removed by a hippy's *juice cleanse* ritual.

Appendix C: New Player Characters

The File of Dread features some of the most unique and well-endowed player characters within the game of L&L. Listed first are the four recommended characters used for tournament play at Glen-Con '23.

Listed next are the stats and descriptions of non-player characters found within the adventure. These NPCs may be used, in addition to the tournament characters, during extensions and side-quests once the adventure concludes.

 Play them all!

Glen Con TOURNAMENT PLAYER CHARACTERS

Utah Spicolli, 1st level surfer

Spicolli is a native-born San Deegan and thus brings a variety of skills to tournament or casual play. He is familiar with local slang, some jargon and is fluent in both *Eng-lish* as well as *Dude*.

Spicollis carries his 6-6 "trusty" Rusty surfboard with him wherever he goes, as this is his pride, joy and also a human toy. Until this adventure, he has never kissed a potential breeding partner, but enjoys hanging out where they might congregate. He spends most of his time at Mission Beach, and will never hesitate to prevent a calamity from befalling his fellow humans, or the ocean which he loves.

Play Utah Spicolli if you are interested in being a human with a short attention span, have little to no interest in *malls* or *shopping*, and wish to battle humungous waves.

Alignment: Lawful Playful Social Class: 9

Drama Rating: 5* vs. high tide, 1

Save vs. bankruptcy: *6*   Save vs. snackage: *10*

Debate Points: *9*

Class Features: speak *Dude* fluently (at will), *stokage, societal chill, inherent reputation*

Social Awareness and Etiquette: 9

Emotional Intelligence: 13

Rhetoric: 6   Logic: 12

Work Ethic: 17   Attractiveness and Health: 12

Equipment: *board of Sur Fing,* wax, *block of sunning*

Garments: surf trunks, flip flops, *tee shirt of rock band,* Haw Wine shirt

Special Abilities, Defenses or Debate Tactics: *local slang, surf chill, legit, proficiency with boards*

Kaitlyn Jacoby (and her familiar, **Meyers**), 1st level logic-user, *law assistant*

Kaitlyn Jacoby has a shadowy past but a bright human smile and personality. Of what we do know, we can say that she survived a grueling test of her mental endurance in the legal towers of Harf Vard. Returning to San Deego after this mighty quest, Kaitlyn Jacoby travels to various hamlets searching for ways to improve the lives of other humans by gifting them with her baked goods and legal advice. She is known to frequent libraries and other localities where tomes and scrolls of knowledge can be found, especially as they pertain to human policy and regulation. Kaitlyn is never without the trusty companionship of her orange feline familiar, Meyers.

Play Kaitlyn if you want to stop opponents dead in their tracks with the use of *factual logic*, if you want to *read logical runes*, or if you want to purvey delicious hipster-inspired treats known as *brownies* (see Humans and History for the connection of these treats to fairy folk in our world).

Alignment: *Chaotic Purposeful* Social Status: *6*

Drama Rating: 4 *political debates, 1*

Save vs. bankruptcy: 8

Save vs. snackage: 14

Debate Points: *9*

Class Features: *jargon, legaleze, rhetorical verbage*

Social Awareness and Etiquette: 10

Emotional Intelligence: 13

Rhetoric:11   Logic:17

Work Ethic: 15   Attractiveness and Health: 16

Equipment: scrolls of human legal knowledge x2, Meyers the Cat (familiar, see Man Manual or Female Folio)

Garments: all-purpose blue business attire with matching blazer and trousers, white colllar shirt, *pen of clicking, pad of noting*

Special Abilities: Defenses or Debate Tactics: *legaleze (DC 12), FEAT: gluten-free dessert ability (DC 11), read human runes, avoid arrest or detention (DC13)*

Spencer McAdams, 1st level hipster

When McAdams was just a child, his mother was a merchant who sold human undergarments at a small *re-tail* store, and his father was a merchant who sold human delicacies from a wheeled beastmount. As McAdams grew to human adolescence he began to help his father sell the marvelous consumables.

Through a small hole in the belly of the beast, McAdams would prepare the morsels and then shout to human buyers, "Take!" Almost always, the humans would then take a bite of the preparation and shout, "Oh!" The McAdams Take-Oh! was thus born, which later became known in colloquial terms as a *tahk-oh*.

In later years, Spencer left his small hamlet in search of a perfect beverage that would match the realistic effects of his tahk-ohs. One day thereafter, he would discover craft beer, and discover his life's mission to seek, consume, and to share amazingly prepared food with the goodly folk of the real realm far and wide.

Play Spencer McAdams if you want to search for consumable or logical items of a savory or fascinating nature, enjoy making the real world a better place with good food and good company, or if you wish to crush your enemies with "world class" charceuterie plates complete with those little utensils so they "don't even have to use their hands."

Drama Rating: *8, 2 in isolation*

Save vs. bankruptcy: 10

Save vs. snackage: 7

Debate Points: *14*

Abilities: *identify organics, create vaca dough, locate natural ingredients*

Social Awareness and Etiquette: 17

Emotional Intelligence: 15

Rhetoric: 7   Logic: 11

Work Ethic: 13   Attractiveness and Health: 12

Equipment: beard conditioner, cock's tail kit

Garments: skin-tight blue jeans, *tee-shirt of rhetorical humor, socks of rhetorical humor*, glasses without lenses

Special Abilities, Defenses or Debate Tactics: *wall of froth* x1 per day, *beer knowledge* at will, *perfect pour* x2, *vaca dough expertise, hipster debate (class skill DC 13), identify hipster, hipster presence* (immediate reaction, x1/day), *aura of patronization and uncomfortability* x1/day (DC12)

Selena Dominguez, 2nd level unemployed therapist, 1st level surfer

Boasting an impressive 18 to her attractiveness and health, Selena Dominguez is a mixture of the obvious and the discreet. Currently, she is employed at the Tiki Mermaid, and is Matilda's "right or left hand girl."

Selena was *rap charmed* into dating dea jay Lazlo and *surf charmed* into dating Deuce Brockit, however Selena soon broke both charms and has instead focused on her surfing and studies in the social and emotional spheres of logic.

She boasts an impressive array of talents, not least of which is that she knows how to guide a mountbeast to her bidding.

Play Selena if you wish to use *eyes of danger*, *eyes of seduction*, or *eyes of "whatthefuck."* Play Selena Dominguez if you wish to protect the more innocent humans of the realm of Merrah Kah from those with *affluence, mingling,* or *nepotism* powers. Play Selena if you wish to help fellow adventurers socially or emotionally and if your sworn enemy is the narcissistic class.

Alignment: Neutral Purposeful
Social Class: 5

Drama Rating: 8

Save vs. bankruptcy: 16

Save vs. snackage: 15

Debate Points: *21*

Abilities: *surf chill* (at will), *reputation enhancer* x3/daily, 10' radius, *Span Lish, license of driving*

Social Awareness and Etiquette: 14

Emotional Intelligence: 16

Rhetoric: 5   Logic: 12

Work Ethic: 11   Attractiveness and Health: 18*

Equipment: *board of sur-fing, wax of sexing*

Garments: *toob top, booty shorts, wetsuit of instant attractiveness (spring)*

Special Abilities, Defenses or Debate Tactics: *eyes of seduction, eyes of oh-shit, eyes of whatthefuck, eyes of danger, flying chanklah, license to drive, cure emotional light woundsx2, male ego restoration x1 (daily), surf chill, proficiency with boards*

NON-PLAYER HUMANS (NPHs)

Bart, Level 5 Conspiracy Theorist

Barthalomew "Bart" Henderson is a uniquely gifted human. Currently he habitates in the corpse of a massive yellow beastmount behind the place of his employment, the Seven to Eleven at "G" and "Olive" streets in the heart of San Deego.

As a powerful conspiracy theorist, bart possesses a swath of strong powers which he uses to pluck information from the nether that typical humans simply cannot detect. He is immune to logic, reasoning and has resistance against factual logic. He is skilled in rhetorical questions, counter-arguments, and self-research.

Play Bart Henderson if you wish to gain access to rumors which are either true or false, wish to avoid logical attacks, and if you enjoy taping pieces of paper to your walls.

Alignment: Lawful Playful Social Class: 9

Drama Rating: 5* vs. high tide, 1

Save vs. bankruptcy: *6*

Save vs. snackage: *10*

Debate Points: *9*

Abilities: *weave story* (DC 11), resistance to marijuana, male ego attacks, logic, vulnerable to *rhetoric* and hemp products

Social Awareness and Etiquette: 7

Emotional Intelligence: 5

Rhetoric: 18   Logic: 8

Work Ethic: 15   Attractiveness and Health: 12

Equipment: *smart foan of believing, scroll of proof against logic x3, hat of telepathic prevention,* hemp necklace, Doctor Bronner's Soap

Garments: Seven to Eleven uniform, sandals

Special Abilities, Defenses or Debate Tactics: *avoid logic* (at will), *conspiracy connection x2, obscure reason x2, conspiracy charm*

Deuce Brockit, "The Rocket", Level 7 Surfer, Level 2 narcissist

Deuce Brockit, also known as The Surf Rocket, is a legend on and off the sand in San Deego. Deuce hails from the great seaside village of Card-dif, where he spent most of his childhood either in the water catching waves, or stealing the hats of beachgoers from the safety of his swiftly moving board of Skay Ting.

Deuce Brockit appears to be very nonchalant, but secretly he harbors a great insecurity, as well as a desire to become Selena's breeding partner again. He believes that his prowess in the ocean is unmatched and that on land he has no rival either.

Play Deuce Brockit if you want to create henchmen and followers through *surf charm*, and *narcissistic patronization*, if you like roleplaying the human ego, and if you have a limited attention span.

Alignment: Lawful Playful Social Class: 9

Drama Rating: 5* vs. high tide, 1
Save vs. bankruptcy: *6*

Save vs. snackage: *10*

Debate Points: *9*

Class Abilities: *stokage, advanced dude, surf chill*

Social Awareness and Etiquette: 15

Emotional Intelligence: 8

Rhetoric: 15   Logic: 13

Work Ethic: 10   Attractiveness and Health: 17

Equipment: *board of shredding +3,* wax of sexing, *trucker hat of indifference, sunglasses of scanning*

Garments: surf trunks, flip flops, *tee shirt of rock band,*

Special Abilities, Defenses or Debate Tactics: *local slang, surf chill, legit, proficiency with boards, toxic masculinity x2, cure serious reef wounds, circle of narcissism (DC15)*

Matilda, Level 3 bartender

The bartender class has always been a mandatory part of most human parties. Their brews, spirits and other potions known as *cock's tails* heal everything except financial attacks. Matilda is the proprietor and operator of The Tiki Mermaid, the most highly rated and well-known hipster bar in all of San Deego.

Matilda's past however is much more of a mystery. Matilda has never divulged her background with her patrons. Instead she chooses to hear the tales of others over a good brew. How Matilda acquired the Tiki Mermaid is one of the most common rumors around, but to this date no one really knows the answer to that question except for Matilda.

Play Matilda if you wish to inspire others around you, if you want to develop reputation auras, or if you wish to solve debates in style without losing a single drop from a good brew.

Alignment: Lawful Playful Social Class: 9

Drama Rating: 5* vs. high tide, 1

Save vs. bankruptcy: 6

Save vs. snackage: *10*

Debate Points: *9*

Abilities: *detect stupidity* (at will), *detect drunkenness (*at will)*, detect lie x2, perfect pour* (at will), *create potion, greater* (at will), *creepbegone!* (immediate reaction x1 daily)

Social Awareness and Etiquette: 6

Emotional Intelligence: 15

Rhetoric: 8   Logic: 11

Work Ethic: 18   Attractiveness and Health: 13

Equipment: Matilda owns a wide array of beer making equipment and a vast inventory of alcoholic beverages in glass bottles

Garments: suit slacks, tennis shoes, *apron of many items, ring of dontbothermejerkweed*

Special Abilities, Defenses or Debate Tactics: *local slang, legit, proficiency with food and drink, server sense x3, purify rhetoric and logic, aura of getthefuckout* (x1/daily)

Ted From Accounting, Level 2 Office Manager

Office Managers come in many shapes and sizes but their primary goals are the same-to create fish'n'sea wherever they go.

Ted From Accounting is a fine example of what a human can do when they are using a fish'n'sea. Ted was only a small human when his father brought him into an annual ritual among the San Deegan nobility. In this secret elitist ritual, parents take their children to their places of work, and when Ted saw his father's office, he knew then what his life's purpose would be.

Play Ted if you are interested in finding out how to create auras among humans that help them to use their abilities together. Play Ted if you want to blend in to any human crowd through sheer lack of a personality and if you want to save money by consuming only food items from *machines of vending*.

Alignment: Lawful Playful Social Class: 9

Drama Rating: 5* vs. high tide, 1

Save vs. bankruptcy: *6*

Save vs. snackage: *10*

Debate Points: *9*

Abilities: *detect donut* (at will), *detect work* (at will), *create excuse* x2/day

Social Awareness and Etiquette: 16

Emotional Intelligence: 4

Rhetoric: 13   Logic: 16

Work Ethic: 7   Attractiveness and Health: 7

Equipment: *gift card of brown-nosing*, vacation calendar, *photo of innocent child* x2

Garments: *suit of sophistication, file folder of ambiguity*, black shoes

Special Abilities, Defenses or Debate Tactics: *office politics, locate office product, zone of jargon, slow work* x2

Chad, Level 3 Preppy: Tennis Coach

When Chad was just a small child living in Lahhoya, his parents took him on their large sea vessel known as a *yot* to a land where other humans did not have time or money for activities like tennis. This affected him greatly as a young human and is the core reason why his character background is now a mix of a subclass of *narcissist* and *local preppy*. Chad's primary objective is to "live his best life" and help those interested in the game of tennis. If these primary objectives cannot be fulfilled, Chad will seek to help himself learn the game of golf, purchase real estate, or establish *passive income* from *influencer* work. No one knows Chad's family name, because Chad does nothing of importance requiring him to tell it to anyone.

Play Chad if you wish to hit a strange looking netted stick against a ball repeatedly, or if you wish to use cunning and tactics to convince others about how important the game of tennis is.

Alignment: Lawful Playful Social Class: 9

Drama Rating: 5* vs. high tide, 1

Save vs. bankruptcy: *6*

Save vs. snackage: *10*

Debate Points: *9*

Abilities: *preppy aura* (5' radius), *create empathetic situation x2,*

Social Awareness and Etiquette: 18

Emotional Intelligence: 5

Rhetoric: 6   Logic: 6

Work Ethic: 4   Attractiveness and Health: 17

Equipment: tennis racket, *balls of accuracyx6,* little black notebook, smart foan

Garments: brand name sneakers, brand name shorts, brand name collar shirt, sunglasses

Special Abilities, Defenses or Debate Tactics: *generate passive income, mingle, influencer x1/day, license of driving*

Appendix D: Suggestions for Future Play

The Rocket's Revenge

Deuce Brockit won his 6th Grand Champion Surf Trophy recently. Even better, the entire scene at South Mission Beach watched him score the last wave, and even worse, save his rival from a total wipe-out! But his moment of perfect glory was then ruined when his potential breeding partner, none other than Selena Dominguez, rejected him for the upstart Utah Spicolli.

Now, Spicolli has made a name for himself on dry land, and all of the humans at The Tiki Mermaid scene have been calling him, not The Rocket, the big *kah-huna* in town. But The Rocket has no intention of drawing a line between his hard-earned turf, and that of Spicolli's new henchmen.

When a new tournament poster comes to the Tiki Mermaid, Spicolli and his party must decide whether or not to enter. But they may not have a choice, because Brockit plans to bring the tsunami directly to Spicolli, no matter how far in the valley he tries to hide. Featuring a new class of narcissist called *internet influencer*, and a new local villain, *seh-gway riders*, this side-quest is sure to keep the adventure in San Deego crashing like waves on a beach.

A Not-so-grand Reopening

*The Law Fir*m of Minick and Minick was closed due to imp priety, as we all now know. And years have passed since a file of any kind was opened in the once sunlit sinister lair of the devel-*lopers.*

But estate is very real in San Deego, and even more so in the village of Lah-hoya. One day, while Kaitlyn Jacoby is searching the upscale shops for cat treats for Meyers, she comes across a scroll, posted in the window of a store. There is to be a grand re-opening of the strip mall in which the devel-lopers once kept their foul lair. But how can this be? Financial codes were established, legaleze was spilled cons*ecrating the ground as holy forever.*

When Kaitlyn Jacoby asks for a few friendly henchmen to disguise themselves and attend the so-called grand re-opening hoping to obtain legal proof of wrong-doing, will you object, or file a motion to answer *her call?*

Low Beer at High Tide

Spicolli and Co. may have closed the file of dread, and saved all of San Deego from disasters both financial and environmental. But how will our heroes handle a *supplychain collapse?* When the local brewmaster runs out of hops, she knows of no one better to contact than the heroes who took on Minick and Minick with a noodle of poodling and a can of effervescently happy snakes.

Featuring a potential showdown with both a *day-trader* and two subclasses of *preppy*, this extension module covers a vast array of real settings from *amoose menparks* to *cruise-ships*.

Will the brew flow once more to the good people who depend on their fermented beverages in San Deego? It takes a dedicated team of human heroes to put together the clues, and the ingredients to solve this mystery.

Bart's Fantastic Bus Voyage

Bart the conspiracy theorist was a large part of the success in defeating the devel-lopers of Lah-hoya. In fact, Bart has become a regular at the Tiki Mermaid, giving friendly advice and information to all these seeking quests in the land of San Deego. But Bart hasn't been around to the Tiki Mermaid in weeks.

When Spencer McAdams brings a case of craft brew to visit his old pal, he'll discover something sinister-Bart's been feeding his wheeled monstrosity which had become his home behind the Seven-to-Eleven. Even worse, the creature has come back from the dead, and can roam the streets like an immense zombie beast!

But Bart claims to have a plan for resurrecting the yellow demon, and when Spencer returns the next day, all he finds is a note. Bart has taken a fantastic bus voyage into the unknown, and McAdams needs your help to find out where he's gone.

An Infestation of Rhetorical Questions

Thanks to the fast-actioned *legaleze* of Kaitlyn and the multi-lingual surfer skills of Utah, the party escaped a coven of powerful carrons at Bahl Boa Park. But while the heroes celebrate, the denizens of *affluency* have been hard at work in the shadows of the city.

With an entire summer to *shmooze* well-connected neighbors and to plan their counterattack, the carrons are ready to spring their trap. And with the power of their combined elitist connections, they won't have to wait by a fountain this time to do it.

Featuring a side quest to a *psai-ance* museum *gift shop*, this adventure boasts a bounty of new logical items for brave heroes such as *witty tee-shirt* and *unsolvable cube puzzle*.

Made in the USA
Middletown, DE
18 September 2023